Stone Skin

The Gargoyles of Arrington, Book 2

Jenn Burke

 Created with Vellum

For Matt, my one and only

Chapter 1

Logan

My SUV's engine sputtered as I passed the *Welcome to Arrington* sign.

Because of course it did.

I slapped my hazards on and checked my mirrors before guiding it over to the shoulder. A semi blasted by me, its horn blaring, and I flinched. Part of me wanted to bear my teeth at the truck driver and give them the finger—but that was a small, almost unrecognizable part of my personality, a piece I rarely let anyone see. Instead, I focused on bringing the SUV to a safe halt, well off the road, and leaned my head against the steering wheel as I put the automatic shift stick into Park.

Fuck.

I didn't need this. I *so* didn't need this. Squeezing my eyes shut against the burning unshed tears, I tried to find the resolve and determination that had kept me functioning for the past six months. That *keep going, no matter what* spirit that had my colleagues praising me and worrying about me in equal measure. Or, well, to be honest, worry more than praise at this point. They all thought I was going to break down.

They weren't wrong.

But not yet. Not yet, dammit. I straightened and swiped at the slight wetness escaping my eyes, then retrieved my cell phone from its holder. This was a simple problem to overcome. Not insurmountable. I'd search for a tow company, and they'd be out to rescue me in no time. Easy.

Except I had no signal. Not a single bar.

"Fuck!" I resisted the urge to throw my phone, that teeth-baring side of me rising once more. I battled it back into place. I was civilized. I didn't lose my temper like this. Not usually, anyway. Settling for tossing my phone onto the passenger seat, I laid my head against the steering wheel and focused on my breathing.

I knew someday soon I would lose it. All those thin strands tethering me to my *keep going* mantra were getting more insubstantial by the week. At first, it had been easy to push all my emotions down because shock had made me numb—it was so much simpler to fall into my work, into my research, and pretend I was fine. But as time crept on, my grief demanded acknowledgment I didn't want to give.

Hence my plan to distract myself by coming to Arrington to hear an Irish legend brought over to the New World by the O'Reilly family. No doubt it was one I'd heard before, but that didn't matter. I hadn't heard this family's spin on it, and each storyteller gave the telling their own flare. It was work but work away from my Vancouver Island home, though not so far I would be stressed out by travel.

In theory. Apparently, in practice, things were different.

I wasn't sure how long I sat there, keeping my breath even and steady and trying not to lose it completely before I caught the telltale sound of tires on gravel. I glanced up to see a tow truck join me on the side of the road. A man exited on the driver's side, wearing worn blue coveralls under a thick fleece-lined red-and-black flannel jacket. He had blond hair peeking out from under the brim of a gray toque and a short, well-groomed brown beard. He blew on his hands and rubbed them together as he walked toward me.

I opened my door and got out to meet him. His steps hesitated slightly as I rose to my full height, a good head taller than he was. Even in my unassuming getup of jeans and a fuzzy burgundy sweater over a pink collared shirt, I knew my size was intimidating. I was six-foot-six, a few pounds shy of three hundred, and everyone I met had a *moment* when they saw me for the first time.

I was used to it. Didn't mean I liked it.

I joined the mechanic at the front of the car, away from the traffic that occasionally buzzed by. The light had waned as I'd wallowed in the SUV—the sun was well behind the trees surrounding us, throwing the area into the gloom of twilight. The temperature had dropped too. At this time of year, the warmth faded quickly when the sun went down. I couldn't begrudge the mechanic his toque and flannel jacket, even if I barely felt the cold.

"Hey!" he greeted me with a smile. "Having trouble?"

I returned his grin with a small uptick of my own lips, nothing near what I would've called a smile. "Yeah. It quit." My lips returned to their normal, downturned state. Lyle had called it my pouty face—

No, not the time to think of him.

"If you can pop the hood, I'll have a look to see if it's something I can fix here and now and get you on your way."

I blew out a breath of relief. "Thanks. How'd you know to come out here, anyway?"

"A friend saw you stopped and let me know. This is a notorious dead zone for cell service."

In no time, the mechanic was leaning under the hood of my SUV, poking and prodding at things I didn't even know the name of. I wasn't too proud to admit I'd never learned the ins and outs of a car's engine. That wasn't my thing.

"So what brings you to Arrington?" he asked as he returned from his truck with a tool. He attached the clamps on it to the SUV's battery.

"Oh, uh...work." I shoved my hands in my pockets. "I'm a professor at UVic."

He glanced at me, something unreadable in his blue gaze, then turned his attention back to the tool in his hand. "There you go. It's your battery."

My shoulders relaxed. "That's a simple fix, right? You can give me a boost and—"

He shook his head. "Not so simple if the battery died while you were driving. That means it's likely the alternator at the root of it."

"Oh." My relief faded like it was never there. I had no idea what an alternator was. "What does that mean?"

The mechanic lowered the hood and made sure it was secure. "It means I give you a tow into my shop, we do some better diagnostics to verify what you need, and I order the part."

"Shit."

He winced, sympathy in his eyes. "Given that tomorrow's Sunday, I won't be able to order anything until Monday at the earliest. But I'd be happy to give you a ride to your hotel. Or wherever you're staying."

"I—" Blinking, I pulled my phone out of my pocket before remembering there was no cell service. Surely I'd booked a hotel? Except my brain was blank whenever I tried to pull up those details. "I don't think I did."

He tilted his head. "You don't think you did what?"

I sighed. "I don't think I booked a hotel."

"Oh." He frowned. "That's not good. There's some sort of convention happening downtown, so rooms might be limited tonight. Are you sure your work didn't—"

"I am my work, and no, I'm pretty sure I didn't. Shit." I scrubbed a hand through my hair. This was not good. "Maybe I can find a spot outside of town."

The mechanic's frown deepened. "Perhaps. But you'll be stuck there all day tomorrow. No car rental places are open on Sunday," he explained.

Ugh. Goddess. Why was my brain like this lately? Well, that was a stupid question. I knew why.

Suddenly, he stuck out his right hand. "Drew O'Reilly."

I took it automatically and shook. His scent wafted over me—clean male sweat, along with hints of stone, metal, oil, and something like...petrichor?

"Logan Davis."

Drew froze. "Professor Logan Davis from the University of Victoria?"

How did he know that? "Yes?"

"Are you perhaps here to see my brother, Rian?"

"Rian O'Reilly is your brother?" I frowned. Drew appeared to be in his thirties, but the email I'd received from Rian had seemed to come from someone much older. His diction was far more formal than I'd expect from a millennial. "Your older brother?"

"Younger, actually." Drew smiled. "He'll be so glad you're here."

A horrible thought washed over me. "I told him I was coming, right?"

"Not as far as I know. He would've been over the moon if he knew." His smile faded, and I could see the wheels turning. First, I hadn't made arrangements for accommodations, and now it seemed I hadn't contacted the person I was here to see to verify they were available. Some professional I was. "Are you all—"

"Fine, fine. Forgetful." I tapped my temple ruefully.

"Sure. It happens to everyone." Something in his eyes told me he didn't quite believe my excuse. "But that makes this a lot easier. We'll tow your SUV in and then you'll come home with me."

"I'll what?"

"I live with my brothers and my partner outside of town. We've got a guesthouse you can stay in. It's no problem, I promise. That way, you won't need a car, and your commute will be about a hundred steps to the main house."

I considered him and his words. It was true that it would be convenient and easy, but I didn't like being dependent on anyone. Though what else was I going to do? Call around to the local hotels once we got to an area with cell service, to confirm they were booked? Because why would Drew lie about that? Besides, if there were any nefarious plots going on at Drew's house, I could always shift to defend myself. Even if it had been months since I'd run as a wolf.

My lips quirked up, as close to a smile as I got these days. "Yeah, sure. Thanks."

Chapter 2

Rian

When I woke, my joints were stiff and my muscles sore. I didn't need to look at my new smartwatch to know I'd slept far longer than I should have.

Again.

Thirty-six hours this time. Not the longest I'd experienced, but that was troubling too. If it had been progressing in a linear pattern, each one of my "naps" getting longer, I could at least plan around it. As it was, I had no idea how long this would go on. For the next two years, until my scheduled sleep in stone? Or would my full sleep unexpectedly come sooner than that?

Five hundred years ago, my brothers and I were cursed. We'd instantly turned into stone gargoyles, and it was only by the grace of our aunt, a gifted witch, that we awoke again at all. She'd modified the curse so we would sleep for a hundred years, wake for twenty-five, and we could permanently break the spell by finding true love. So far, out of the five of us, Finnian and Drew had managed it—Finnian had found Elizabeth a hundred years ago and lived out his human life while we slept, and Drew had realized Josh, our personal assistant and caretaker, was his true love a short month before. Odhrán, our youngest brother, had died while we slept hundreds of years ago. That left Teague and me still searching for a way to break the curse. I didn't think true love was going to be my way out. Not with the clock ticking like it was. But I supposed there was always next time. After I slept through another brother's life.

A shower helped loosen my muscles, even if I couldn't truly feel the hot water on my living stone skin, and washed away most of the fuzziness in my brain. Then I went downstairs to the kitchen to find Josh sitting at the island, drinking coffee.

"Morning," I greeted him.

"Hey." A flash of a relieved smile was the only sign he gave that he'd been concerned. After we'd realized I was starting to fall into long, involuntary naps, my brothers, Josh, and I had decided not to dwell on it. It wasn't going to help, and there was nothing we could do about it. No point in making a fuss. "Want some coffee?"

I rotated my head in a half-circle motion, the weight of my horns familiar and as annoying as ever. "Sure."

Josh hopped off the stool to get me a mug. I took the stool next to Josh's, carefully settling my weight. "What'd I miss?"

"A few sittings."

Ugh, yeah. I'd had four appointments for tattoos set for this week. As soon as I was down for the count, Josh would have called them up and rescheduled. I hated disappointing my clients. "When did you reschedule them to?"

Josh put the mug in front of me and got back up on the gargoyle-strength stool. "Two to January. The other two, Geri took on."

I nodded my approval. Geri, my partner at Rune Ink, was pretty much why I hadn't closed the tattoo shop's doors while I rode out this "nap" nonsense. "Thanks. Anything else?"

"Well...I've got some news."

"You're pregnant."

He rolled his eyes. "Yes. I have defied the laws of nature and, without a uterus, have become pregnant."

I grinned. "You're even starting to sound like Drew."

"Oh, shut up." He bumped his shoulder against mine, looking more than pleased that he was starting to share one of Drew's traits. Not that Drew was too formal when he spoke since we all tried to adapt to the slang and sayings of the time. I still tended to write more formally than I should though.

I sipped my coffee. "So, what's the news?"

"A certain professor showed up last night."

My mug clattered to the table as I set it down—okay, nearly dropped it. "Logan Davis?"

"Yes."

"He's here?"

Josh laughed. "Yes."

I jumped up. "Oh my gods. I need to...I need to..." What? "Get dressed. Saw off my horns. Get into my human skin."

"Eh, a different order would be good."

Right. Skin first, then horns—the stupid things were always there, even when I looked human, so I had to get rid of them daily—and then clothes. Thankfully, sawing down my horns was as painless as trimming my hair or nails. No big deal. I had this. I could be cool. I could forget that this was the man I'd wanted to meet for months, whose picture and biography I'd memorized. I'd finally gotten the courage to reach out to him when I'd woken from my first long nap. I hadn't heard back from him, though, and I'd thought that was that.

Except he was *here*. Now. This wasn't good news—this was *amazing* news. Professor Logan Davis, with his knowledge of folklore and legends, could have the answers we needed on breaking our curse without the stipulation of finding true love.

Josh grabbed my wrist before I could race back to my room to get ready. "Rian..."

His tone and sudden somber expression dampened the excitement running through my veins. "What?"

"There's something up with him." He briefly explained how Drew had found him on the side of the road and how Logan had apparently come to Arrington without booking a hotel or contacting me.

"So he's forgetful. Isn't that a—a meme? The absent-minded professor?"

Josh's lips twisted. "Not a meme, a stereotype."

"Right." Stereotypes were bad. I remembered that much. "I don't really see the problem though."

"You will. When you meet him...you will." Josh sighed. "Want help with your horns?"

"Yes, *please*." The excitement over seeing the man I'd been thinking about for months came rushing back. The sooner I could become presentable as a human, the sooner I could meet him. And hopefully, start puzzling out a way to break this curse forever.

I ADJUSTED my backward hooligan hat to make sure it was on straight, took a breath, and knocked on the door of our guesthouse. The structure was painted in the same color scheme as the main house—a crisp white with black trim, a palette Josh had chosen a few years back to freshen the look of the century-old property. The door I stood in front of, as well as the mansion's front door, was a cranberry red. The artist in me appreciated the color contrast against the trees surrounding the two structures.

The man, though, wondered why Logan wasn't answering the door.

I knocked again and called out a hello for good measure. Nothing.

My smartwatch told me it was close to eleven o'clock. Josh had said Drew had brought Logan to the guesthouse around six the evening before, and despite being invited to the main house for dinner, Logan hadn't shown up. Everyone assumed he'd fended for himself with the well-stocked guesthouse pantry and turned in early, but what if...

Shit. What *if*.

There were a ton of possibilities. He could have slipped in the shower. He could have fallen down the stairs. He could have—gods forbid—hurt himself on purpose. And then there was the mountain lion pride we'd tangled with a few short weeks ago, not to mention the Fomori—the evil fae-like creature who'd killed our parents, cursed us, and returned centuries later to retrieve what she thought she was owed. She was the most dangerous threat of them all.

This time, I pounded on the door, but the spark of panic flaring in my gut wouldn't let me stop there. I tried the door handle, and my heart thudded in my throat when it turned easily. Not locked.

I shoved it open, panic well and truly taking over. "Logan? Logan Davis?"

Heavy steps sounded on the stairs, followed by, "Yeah, yeah. Coming."

Air rushed into my lungs. By the tone, he was fine. Maybe a little muddled, but...

All thoughts fled as I caught sight of Logan Davis in person for the first time. Instead of his hair being neatly combed to the side, as it was in his official photo on the university's website, his dark-blond locks were mussed, standing up at the back of his head and on the left. The picture hadn't done justice to his size, either—the man was easily five or six inches over six feet and built like a soft, cushy tank. His orange T-shirt displayed rolls of padding around his stomach and his pillowy-looking pecs, and his thighs challenged the strength of his black-and-white-checked pajama pants.

He looked like he gave the best hugs.

I shot him a sheepish smile. "Sorry. I knocked."

"I thought I heard something." He rubbed at one hazel eye before opening them wide and blinking a few times, no doubt trying to wake up. "I didn't mean to worry you. I slept really hard last night."

"Fresh mountain air will do that."

"I guess." His lips twitched but never lifted into a true smile. "And you are?"

"Oh! Sorry." I stepped forward, my hand out. "Rian O'Reilly. We shared emails. I can't tell you how happy I am that you're—"

Logan took a step back. "You're not human."

Chapter 3

Logan

I didn't know what Rian O'Reilly was, but he was *definitely* not human.

He was cute though.

Red hair poked out from under a flat cap turned backward, exposing the freckles on his forehead that continued to the tip of his nose and across his cheeks. They made him look young, though he couldn't be that young—maybe thirty? Unless he was the sort of nonhuman with an abnormally long lifespan, in which case he could be hundreds of years old. He dressed like a contemporary to this time, though, wearing athletic pants and a Henley top with the sleeves pushed up, exposing intricate tattoos on his forearms. Some had runes buried within their designs, which was...very interesting.

I couldn't identify what sort of creature he was by scent, though the tang of ozone indicated he certainly had some magic. There was the aroma of stone too, the ancient sort that I'd smelled at various historic sites across Europe and America.

Rian's smile stayed in place, though his blue eyes lost

some of their welcoming sparkle. "Uh...not human?" He chuckled, but it sounded forced. "You sure you're okay, doc?"

So that's how he was going to play it, huh? He wasn't a shifter, or else he'd have sniffed out my wolf side as soon as he walked in the door. I held up a hand and let my inner beast out enough to change my nails to sharp claws. My wolf whined at the hint of freedom.

Soon, I promised him. This was probably the best location for shifting I'd visited in months, if not years, particularly if my hosts weren't human.

He whined again but settled. He was me and I was him, and we trusted each other. When I said soon, I meant it, and he knew it.

Rian's smile had dimmed at my display, but he hadn't run out the door in fear. Uh-huh, as I thought. He knew what he was looking at.

"Werewolf?" he guessed.

"Yep." I returned my hand to normal and held it out for the shake I'd rejected earlier. "Of the Redwoods clan." Not that the overarching clan even acknowledged my existence, but it was better than saying lone wolf.

Which was what I was. Now.

The grief that hadn't gone away for months threatened to overwhelm me, but I refused to let it. Now was not the time. It didn't matter that there never seemed to be a right time, and it didn't matter that I'd acknowledged a few short hours ago that I was heading for a breakdown if I didn't face what I was feeling head-on. Giving in to my grief was a useless, selfish urge. Who and what would it help? No one and nothing. Better to continue pushing forward. To keep living.

That's what they would want.

Rian grasped my hand, and a spark of *something* zapped through my palm at the connection. Some leftover element of his magic, probably, since he gave no indication that he felt anything. Weird, but ultimately unimportant. I took my hand back and resisted the instinct to shake it out. I didn't want him to think I thought he had cooties or something.

Way to revert to your six-year-old self, Logan.

Mentally rolling my eyes at my internal monologue, I gestured at the seating to the left of the door. The guesthouse wasn't big, but it was nicely appointed with everything someone staying here for a short time could want, and I found the furniture big enough for me, which wasn't common in other places I'd stayed. Everything was slightly oversized, and rather than making the space inside the small house feel cramped and tight, it was cozy. Honestly, I'd felt more at home here last night than I had in my condo for months. Maybe it was the quiet plus the proximity of the forest. Now that my wolf had reminded me he needed a run, that made sense.

"Dr. Davis? Uh, Logan?"

I blinked, realizing that while I'd waved Rian to have a seat—in his own bloody guesthouse—I'd zoned out. "Sorry," I said, my lips curving a tad. "No coffee yet."

Rian popped up from the armchair. "You sit. I'll get it."

"No, I—"

"You're my guest, not the other way around. Sit."

Bemused, I followed his order and watched him fuss in the kitchen to get the Keurig going. The main floor was all one space, with the kitchen open to the small dining area and the living room. The walls were varnished pine, broken up by the off-white furniture and pale seafoam-green kitchen cabinets. The overall look was elegant and rustic, a style I'd never considered for my own place. I liked clean, modern lines—or so I'd thought. My condo definitely didn't feel as comfortable as this, though it was aesthetically pleasing.

"You need some color in here." Mom put her hands on her hips and turned slowly to take in the entirety of my new apartment. It was a loft-style, with exposed brick walls, but I'd gone with shiny black modern cabinets in the kitchen, with a concrete countertop, and my choice of furniture was equally as clean.

"Black is a color," I pointed out.

"Black is not a color." She huffed. *"Next, you'll be trying to tell me chrome is a color too."*

"I would never."

"Dr. Davis?"

Another set of blinks. Rian was holding a mug of coffee out to me, which I took, still lost in the memory. I cleared my throat. "Sorry."

Rian waved it off and reclaimed the armchair. At some point in my fugue state, I'd chosen the couch opposite it. There was a sugar bowl and a tiny pitcher of cream on the coffee table between us, but I was happy to take the coffee black.

"You said you slept hard last night, but you..." He drifted off, likely realizing what he was about to ask was far more personal than one would usually get with someone they'd just met.

However, I took it in the spirit he meant it. Concern was woven all through his odd scent. "It's been a rough few months." He could interpret what he would from that, but I wasn't going to expand on it.

Not yet. My brow furrowed, and I quickly corrected it to *not ever.* I wasn't here to be friends with Rian. I was here to learn about the legend he'd hinted at.

"So," I said, leaning back in my seat. "You're not human."

He sipped his coffee, then shook his head. "I used to be, but not since...well." His chuckle held no humor. "Not for a very, very long time."

This time it was easy to identify the spark that flared inside me. It was the one that drove me to find out more about legends and stories. The one that used to be a bonfire in my brain but had dwindled to a barely there flicker. My curiosity hadn't died, but it wasn't the driving force it had once been.

I gestured for Rian to go on, and with a sigh so light I almost missed it, he put his mug down on the coffee table. Next, he swept off his hat and ruffled his red hair, and... there was something buried in the rich locks I couldn't quite make out. My curiosity poked at me to get up and look closer, but then Rian did something I wasn't expecting.

He started taking off his shirt.

That's when I discovered his tattoos didn't stop at his forearms. They traveled up to his shoulders and across his chest and down his abdomen to...

I swallowed and jerked my gaze back up.

He folded the garment into a sloppy bundle and put it aside. "Sorry, but I really like this shirt."

That was all he said before he...changed.

It wasn't truly a shift, not like what I was used to. He was changing forms, shifting in that sense, but the creature who sat on the chair was still Rian. If larger and grayer and made of... living stone?

That explained the heft of the furniture.

And with *horns*. That's what I'd spotted before—the stubs of this set of massive spiral horns that jutted from the top of his head, then curved to either side in line with his temples.

The ink he'd sported on his human skin was gone, except for the runes. They dotted his arms and chest, some of which I recognized but most not. His fingers sported talons that made my claws look like slightly overgrown nails. His red eyes were unsettling, reminding me of demons, though I quickly ruled out that explanation for what he was. Demons had a very specific scent, and Rian's didn't have the telltale sulfuric overtones.

"What...?" I whispered, barely aware I'd spoken aloud.

"I'm a gargoyle." He shifted his head, rolling his neck as though the weight of the horns bothered him. Maybe they did—they weren't small. "About five hundred years ago, my brothers and I were cursed—"

"The legend you hinted at," I guessed, not particularly caring that I'd interrupted him. "But..." I snapped my fingers. "Your brother. The mechanic."

"Drew?"

"He didn't smell nonhuman."

"He broke his curse. He—"

"If you know the origins of the story, and you know how to break the curse, then why am I here?"

His red eyes flared, and the scent of annoyance sharpened his stone-and-ozone aroma. "If you'll let me get out a full sentence, I'll tell you."

Fair. I sat back and gestured for him to continue.

And continue he did. Time fell away as I got caught up in the story he told about the witch—actually a Fomori— who killed their parents, the fact they were given the right to kill her as a way of serving justice, the curse the Fomori cast on them before they could, and the modifications their aunt was able to make that allowed them to wake for twenty-five years after a hundred years asleep and gave them hope they could break their curse by finding true love.

But sustaining that hope was hard. They'd awoken the second time to find their youngest brother dead, his stone form broken into dust. And the time they were awake before now, another of their brothers did break his curse, but that was bittersweet. He'd lived out his human life while they slept and missed out on his life entirely.

I wasn't so numb to the world that the story didn't move me, but I couldn't go so far as to imagine how they'd felt when they had to say goodbye to their brother at the turn of the twentieth century. I knew intimately how torturous saying goodbye to a loved one was, and I didn't want to revisit it.

"We have two years left in this cycle. Two more years awake. In theory."

My brow twitched. "What do you mean by that?"

"There's something wrong with the magic. My older brother, Teague, woke up two years early, and it seems like I might..." He paused as if the next words were hard to say. "I might be going to turn to stone two years early. I'm having long periods of sleep that no one can wake me from."

"How long?"

"Sometimes hours, sometimes days. It's not consistent. If it were, I'd have some idea of whether the time I won't wake up is getting closer, but I don't." He met my eyes. "I don't want to go to sleep again, Dr. Davis. I want to see my brother and Josh get married. I want to share their lives. I want to see Teague find happiness."

I narrowed my eyes as a particular thought became lodged in my brain. "You're not expecting me to be your true love, right?"

That startled a bark of laughter out of Rian, and it was

surprising how much it changed his monstrous visage. In this form, he was nowhere close to what I would call handsome—his brow was too prominent, his nose too long and sharp, and his chin jutted out like a cartoon goblin. But when he smiled, it somehow lit him from inside, erasing the ugly features and revealing the shiny spirit underneath.

"No," he said, still smiling. "Absolutely not. I want your help to find a cure that doesn't involve true love. Depending on true love to show up in the next two years, or sooner...it leaves too much to chance. There has to be something else we can do. I've tried runes—"

"Those are yours?" I levered myself out of my seat as he held out an arm marked with designs. Without thinking, I grabbed it so I could examine it. Vaguely I noted his skin was cooler than mine or a human's but not as cold as true stone. It was surprisingly supple too, though a hardness underneath illustrated this man was definitely not human. "This is ogham, correct?"

"Yes." His voice had a puzzled tone as I turned his arm to see the other designs. "Can you read it?"

I tilted my head from side to side. "I recognize some of the letters, but I'm no expert at translating them." I pointed to a set of four diagonal lines with a horizontal line cast through them. "This is ruis. Meaning...red, I believe?"

"On its own. But I've combined it with—" He indicated two other symbols, their names rolling off his tongue so naturally and quickly I couldn't follow. Ancient Irish was not my area of study. "With the three of them together, my intention was to cancel the red. Meaning to end the magic that makes my eyes so awful." His lips twisted into a self-deprecating smirk. "Obviously, it didn't work."

"Interesting. So you've carved runes on yourself in an attempt to beat the curse?"

"Tattooed," he corrected. "They appear as carvings in this form, but they're actually tattoos I made on my human skin. My nonmagical tattoos don't appear in this form at all." He turned slightly and indicated his back, which was bare of ink. "The tattoo artist I apprenticed with did a back piece for me of all my brothers and me. Our silhouettes in front of a sunset. I kind of hate it disappears when I'm in this form—I always worry it will be gone when I take on my human skin again."

"That's fascinating. I've never seen anything like it." I turned his arm again and pointed to a rune on the inside of his biceps. "This one isn't an ogham letter, is it?"

"No. That's, uh, something I made up."

Something in his tone encouraged me to glance at his face, and I could swear there was a rosy undertone to his cheeks that wasn't there before. Huh, gargoyles could blush. I cataloged that away to be ruminated on later and turned my attention back to the design. "What was your intention with this one?"

"It's for protection. I can activate it with a touch, and it hardens my skin close to actual stone."

I didn't ask him to demonstrate, but I was very tempted. I had no talent for magic, never had—other than shifting into my wolf form—and every time I witnessed true magic, it intrigued me.

Rian swept a claw over the design, not triggering it. "Before this time awake, before I discovered tattooing, I used to write runes on slips of paper, but they never worked. No, I shouldn't say never. Sometimes they worked."

"Oh?" As much as I wanted to keep examining his runes, I returned to my seat, eager to hear about the *sometimes* his runes worked.

He absently stroked a hand over one of his horns, like a

normal human might swipe a hand through their hair when slightly embarrassed. "It was my aunt who encouraged me to start learning the art. I never clued in that she was a true witch though." He shook his head. "Looking back, it should have been obvious."

"Hindsight is twenty-twenty." The words popped out of my mouth, something my mom used to say, and for a second, I couldn't even swallow.

Rian didn't seem to notice. "True. When we first awoke after the curse, we couldn't take on our mostly human form, which was terrifying. It was the seventeenth century, and everyone still believed in monsters, which made going into towns for supplies difficult, to say the least. But we were still alive. We still needed to eat. I drew an ogham rune on my cloak to hide my features, and it worked. After that, I continued experimenting. I'd say my runes work about half the time."

I was silent for a moment, pushing the flash of grief aside while I parsed out the conundrum of Rian's runes. "Are your personal designs more or less effective than the ogham?"

"I haven't made up a lot of designs, to be honest."

"But the ones you have, do they work?"

"I—yes?" He paused, the glow of his red eyes dimming for a moment before flaring, brighter than before. "Yes. Holy shit. Always."

I allowed my lips to curve at the corners. "Ogham is not inherently esoteric in nature. It's simply a very old way of communicating. You have the power to imbue your own designs with the magic needed to make them effective, but I'm going to guess you were focusing on the ogham because it's ancient and the first thing you learned, yes?"

Rian sank back into the chair, stunned. "Why didn't I see that before?"

"Sometimes when we're too close to something, we can't see it."

"Can't see the forest for the trees, eh?" He smiled again, the expression surprisingly light for someone facing a time limit. "Doc, you're amazing."

Heat rushed to my cheeks, and I shrugged. "You can call me Logan."

"Logan, then."

I shivered. Why did my name sound so good coming from his lips?

Chapter 4

Rian

I t was still weird to see Drew as a human working on his projects at home. Normally, he'd be in his living stone form since that was easiest for us to maintain—except now he didn't have one of those. After realizing Josh was his true love, he was one hundred percent human. Other than the magic that allowed him to manipulate metal, which he was using right now to restore an old car part. What it was, I had no idea.

I leaned against the wall in the garage. The doors were open, letting in the crisp late-autumn air I barely felt. I wore athletic pants for modesty but nothing else, my living stone skin exposed to the elements. Drew was in a pair of coveralls over a long-sleeve thermal shirt. While he focused on his work, I watched the last colors of the sunset fade into twilight. But instead of appreciating them fully, my thoughts were consumed by Logan Davis.

I opened my mouth to say something to Drew about him when I heard tires crunching over the driveway gravel. I stiffened for a second, ready to duck back inside, but quickly recognized Teague's car as it appeared around the bend. Good timing. We might as well discuss it as a family.

"Where's Josh?"

Drew, who'd been watching Teague's approach, placed the hunk of metal on his workbench. "Out with Em to some sort of fancy charity dinner."

"And you let him go alone? You're growing as a person, brother."

"Trasna ort féin."

I laughed at the *go fuck yourself* said with such love. "Seriously, though. You're not worried?"

Josh, our personal assistant, had been a favorite target of the mountain lion pride running rampant across Arrington a month ago. He'd nearly died at one point, and for a while, I'd thought Drew would never let the man out of his sight again. But the lions appeared to have gone to ground, and Drew was working with a therapist to deal with his reaction to Josh's near-death experience.

I was honestly, truly proud of him.

"Dr. Pierre says I need to build my trust again—of Josh, of the world in general." The hunk of metal in front of him suddenly shimmered, wavered, and melted before solidifying into an unrecognizable lump. He let out a sigh. "It's a work in progress."

Teague pulled up to the working garage rather than parking in his usual spot next to the one we used for our vehicles. When he got out of the cruiser, he was still wearing his uniform and looking very much like the tired police officer he was. His shirt was rumpled instead of having the sharp creases he started out every shift with, and there was some unidentifiable substance on one sleeve. His eyes bore the shadows of a long day being bombarded with emotions.

Ever since we were cursed, we'd all demonstrated some inherent magic. I had my runes, Drew had his metal, and Teague could sense emotions. Usually, he kept himself as closed off to them as possible, presenting as stoic and unaffected, but I knew it wasn't the core truth of who he was. My eldest brother felt deeply and hard—he only pretended he didn't.

Today's shift must have been especially difficult if he looked this worn out. "Rough day?"

He grunted and went straight to the fridge Drew kept in his workspace to retrieve a beer. After popping the top on the tallboy can, he downed a few large swallows and immediately let out a belch worthy of any monster. "Excuse me. Yeah. It was...not fun."

I waited. Sometimes Teague shared, sometimes he didn't. When he experienced things that were particularly difficult, it could go either way. He was, after all, a stoic bastard.

"We got a call for an accidental drowning in the creek in the Sitka Grove subdivision," he said after a full minute of silence.

"Oh shit," I breathed.

"It was the mother who found him. A six-year-old boy who'd been playing near the creek with his friend. He slipped on rocks and knocked his head, then fell into the water. The friend ran to the boy's house and...yeah." He took another long swallow of his beer. "When I got there, the mom was trying to do CPR, but she was so panicked. So terrified."

"Please tell me you resuscitated him."

Finally, there was a shadow of a smile. The barely there twitch of lips reminded me so much of Logan that I was stunned for a second. Since when had the professor settled himself so firmly in my thoughts?

"Yeah, we did," Teague said. "He was awake and crying when they loaded him into the ambulance. But the mother's emotions..." He shuddered.

"Glad it was a happy ending." Drew got a beer out of the fridge, opened it, and handed it to me before getting another for himself. I appreciated that he opened mine—talons got in the way of opening beer cans neatly.

We tapped our cans together in a salute to the boy who'd survived. Not all of Teague's stories had such a good outcome. The nature of police work, I supposed.

Teague's violet-tinged blue eyes looked me over. "Good to see you up and about."

When he'd left this morning, I was still enjoying one of my "naps."

"Did you meet our houseguest?"

"I did. He's not what I expected."

"Right?" Drew said. "He's not entirely there, is he? And I don't mean that in a derogatory way. He's just not present a lot of the time."

"You're right. He isn't," I agreed. "He's also a werewolf."

"You scut, he's not."

"Yes, he is," I countered Drew with a laugh. "He caught on that I wasn't human right away and showed me his claws so I'd know what he was."

"Huh." Teague took a seat on one of the hefty folding chairs Drew kept for us. "I suppose it makes sense that a professor researching legends might be one of those legends himself."

Well, when he put it that way... "He recognized my runes too. Said the ogham isn't inherently magical, which is why they might not work all the time."

"Didn't I tell you that? I'm *sure* I told you that," Drew crowed.

"When?"

"I don't know. Sometime in the 1700s?"

"You did not."

"I am *positive* I did. But no, you wouldn't listen to your big brother—"

"Children, children," Teague interrupted. We flipped him off in unison, and he chuckled. "Did you find out anything about him?"

"What do you mean?" I carefully tipped a sip of beer into my mouth, having mastered drinking with this stupid nose and chin centuries ago.

"Why he's so mentally absent."

"Not really. I didn't want to invade his privacy." I shrugged. "Why, what did you feel?"

"A whole lot of nothing, honestly." Teague frowned. "It was as though he was disconnected from his emotions, which fits his mental absence. Like he's disassociated from that part of himself. It's not good."

"But is that our business?" Drew gestured to the three of us with his can. "We don't know him. We can't force him to share with us."

Teague raised a brow. "He's a dissociative werewolf living in our guesthouse."

Drew tipped his can in Teague's direction. "Okay. Fair point."

"So what do we do about it?" I asked.

Drew smirked. "I think by *we*, you mean *you*."

I opened my mouth to protest that it should be a group effort, but Teague spoke before I could. "Drew's right. He barely said a handful of words to Drew and me, but with you, he had a whole conversation. And let's not forget he's here on your invitation."

There *was* that. Neither of my brothers needed to know that I'd sort of—okay, not sort of, *actually*—obsessed over Logan's picture on the UVic website. Spending more time in Logan's company certainly wouldn't be a hardship. But I had no idea how to draw him out of his shell.

My uncertainty must have come through to Teague because his expression softened into something more sympathetic. "Spend time with him. Talk to him. It doesn't always have to be about his work. Maybe what he really needs is a vacation."

A vacation. I pondered that idea. There were plenty of things to do in Arrington, especially for someone with an intrinsic connection to nature as a werewolf. "I could introduce him to Chris."

It seemed as though Teague's eyes flared more purple than his human eyes should at the mention of the alpha who led the werewolf pack tied to our family, but that had to be a trick of the fluorescent lighting in the garage. "You could," Teague said, his voice even.

Drew grunted. He didn't particularly like the MacGrath pack—long ago, we'd had bad blood with them that he wasn't over. To be truthful, I wasn't either, but I hid it better. "That might not be a bad idea. He can run with them or whatever they do."

"Excellent. We have a plan." I tapped my can against my brothers' again.

"One more thing," Teague said. "We had a mountain lion sighting tonight."

THE IRONY of being me was that I didn't need a lot of sleep. Regular sleep, anyway. Neither did my brothers—well, Drew was human now, but before. It was one of the reasons we were able to make so much of our twenty-five years awake.

After Teague's bombshell that the mountain lion pride was back—maybe—I definitely wasn't going to sleep. I sat on the back patio in my stone skin, sketch pad on the table in front of me, a thick, sturdy pencil in my right hand. I preferred sketching in my human form, but it became harder to hold on to that skin after dark. Besides, I'd need more light and heat because as temperate as British Columbia was, it still got damn cold overnight in early December. It hadn't snowed yet, but there was a hint of it in the air, that scent of imminent precipitation and bone-deep chill that meant more than rain was on the way. The pine and fir trees surrounding our property were dark sentinels against the night sky, and I felt completely safe despite the possible reemergence of the pride's threat. It was Drew and Josh I worried about.

And, all right, Logan too.

He didn't know about the trouble we'd had, so he was vulnerable, despite being a werewolf. Not that I thought the pride would attack us on our property—they'd tried that once, and it hadn't worked out well for them. If—when— they struck again, it would be something new. Sneakier. I gave up on anticipating what they might do since I was no criminal mastermind. My creativity leaned toward art, not brainstorming new and frightening ways to hurt people.

I sighed when I refocused on my sketch pad and realized I'd drawn a mountain lion. They were impressive, gorgeous creatures...right up until they tried to kill you. I lifted a hand to tear out the page and scrunch it into a ball but decided against destroying it. The subject might not be one I would have chosen consciously, but it was good work. Time for me to head inside before I managed to magically summon the pride somehow.

But maybe I'd walk around the house first to check.

I tucked my sketch pad under my arm and headed around the side of the house closest to the guesthouse. Every window in the guesthouse glowed with warm, welcoming light, which would be great if it weren't past three in the morning. What was Logan still doing up? Before I knew it, my feet had taken me to the guesthouse's front door, which I tapped with a knuckle. When I got no response, I tried the knob, and, of course, it was unlocked.

Dammit. I would have to tell Logan about the pride's possible return so he'd take more care.

I was about to call Logan's name when I saw him sitting at the small dining table. His dark-blond hair was in disarray, as though he'd swept his hands through it more than once and hadn't realized he'd messed it up quite thoroughly. He wore the same orange T-shirt I'd seen him in this morning, paired with the same black-and-white-checked pajama pants. There were papers spread across the flat surface—he'd discovered the printer hidden in the upstairs closet—and he was staring at his laptop with eyes reddened from strain and fatigue. For once, I wished I had Teague's ability to sense emotions—it would be great to have some insight into what drove Logan. Why was he up at oh-dark-thirty?

"Logan," I said, moderating my voice in the hope of not startling him.

"Hm?" he responded, not even looking away from his screen.

I stepped fully into the room and closed the door behind me. "What are you doing?"

"Working." The *can't-you-see* in his voice was subtle, like all his emotions, but there.

"Right. But why?"

That did make him look up. "You asked for my help."

"Yes, but I don't want you to wear yourself out."

He blinked at me, silent, as though those words made no sense. And maybe they didn't. How long had he been awake? When was the last time he'd eaten?

"You should go to bed."

He turned back to his screen, the blue light etching the shadows under his eyes even deeper into his pale skin. "In a minute. It's not even that late."

I frowned, placing my sketch pad on the table over one of his papers. I had a feeling I might need both hands to convince him to abandon his work for the night. "Logan, it's past three in the morning. It's definitely late."

He looked up again, this time to check the windows. When he saw the darkness, he said, "Huh." Then he frowned at me. "Why are you still up?"

"I don't need as much sleep as humans. Or were-wolves." I reached over the table and closed his laptop. "C'mon. Sleeping time."

"I was—" A giant yawn cut off whatever he was about to say. When it finished, he looked absolutely exhausted. "Yeah. Okay." He got up from the table, then paused. "You won't touch anything, right?"

"I won't. I promise." Remembering Teague's suggestion that Logan might be in dire need of a vacation, I continued, "But you're going to leave it alone tomorrow."

"What? No. I need to read—"

"You need a break. Tomorrow, we'll go on a tour of Arrington." It came out with more confidence than I felt, seeing as I'd decided on it right then. "It'll be a good refresh."

The corners of his mouth tightened. "We don't really have time for that kind of break."

I shrugged. "I don't think a few hours will make that big of a difference in the long run. I'll be back after lunch, all right? I want you to sleep for at least that long."

"That's nine hours."

"More like eight and a half, and you look like you could use double that." Blunt, yes, but I felt Logan needed some bluntness. He did *not* look good, and I was beginning to suspect he wasn't the best at taking care of himself.

He pressed his lips together for a second. "Fine. I'll stay in bed until noon."

I noticed he didn't say he'd sleep, but I let it go. Baby steps. "And make sure you eat something when you get up."

He rolled his eyes. "I *am* an adult, you know."

I said nothing, refusing to take back my order.

"*Fine.* I'll eat something. Should I take a picture and send it to you as proof?"

"Sure." I grinned, a small spurt of happiness rushing through me when he didn't flinch at my horror-movie visage. It could have been that he was too tired to react, but whatever. I'd take it.

He sighed. "I don't need a keeper."

I said nothing, simply looked at the table covered with papers and back to him.

His shoulders slumped. "I'll see you after lunch," he relented.

"Looking forward to it."

I really was.

Chapter 5

Logan

Main Street was what I'd expected to see in an older town like Arrington. While the rest of the city had embraced the twentieth and twenty-first centuries, this stretch along the river was still firmly ensconced in the nineteenth. Some of the buildings were made of stone, but most were wood, sporting false façades and old-fashioned signs. They were painted in modern colors—bright, eye-catching hues that weren't authentic to the period they were built but gave the street a happy, welcoming vibe.

Much like what the man walking beside me was projecting.

It was obvious that Rian loved this town. He had stories for every store we passed, some from recent memory and some from when the buildings were first erected. He was a hand-talker, gesturing to emphasize everything he said. At one point, he knocked his backward hat askew and quickly righted it before it could fall off and reveal his horn stubs.

He gave me a sheepish look and tamed his hands. "Whoops."

"Do you— How do you—" I didn't know how to ask what I wanted to know, so I waved at his hat.

"Handsaw. Whenever I decide I'm human for the day." He shrugged. "It doesn't hurt. It's like trimming your nails."

"How annoying."

"I'm used to it." He glanced at the window of the store next to us. "Oh hey, let's check this one out. You'll like it."

Considering I wasn't a big shopper when I was in the best of moods—and I certainly wasn't in one of my better frames of mind—I doubted I would like anything. But I trailed in Rian's wake as he entered the store, an old-fashioned bell twinkling overhead. In the back of my brain, I wondered why I was humoring him. He'd asked me here to do a job, one I was fully capable of doing, and staying in bed until noon and touring the town wasn't part of it. I didn't even know why he cared. We weren't friends. We weren't even work colleagues. We were little more than strangers.

Except, then I caught sight of the store he'd led me into.

It was an antique store of a sort. But instead of being filled with furniture, this one had shelves upon shelves of books, trinkets, and curiosities. The acrid aroma of *old* perfumed the air—astringent notes of aged wood, the mustiness of brittle paper, and the layers of generations who had held these items and soaked their individual scents into them.

I gazed around the store in awe, not only because of its uniqueness but because Rian had nailed it. This was exactly the sort of store I liked. Antique stores in general, but my condo didn't have room for all the furniture I ended up wanting to buy, so I avoided bruising my heart by not going into them. But this place, with its little treasures—I could browse to my heart's content and take home whatever I liked.

"Cool, right?" Rian grinned, his wide smile much more appealing in his human form than his gargoyle but no less bright and charming.

"Very cool." My lips twitched at his obvious pleasure in sharing this place with me, but they didn't tip into an actual smile.

His grin widened as he made a *yes!* fist pump. "I knew you'd like it."

"Welcome to Curios." A surprisingly young-sounding female voice preceded its owner through the maze of shelves. An instant later, the woman came into view. She wasn't nearly as young as her childlike voice suggested. I guessed her to be in her late twenties. Dark-wash denim jeans hugged her slender frame, paired with a silky-looking cream blouse, a russet blazer, and brown leather ankle boots. She had long, wavy brown hair highlighted with delicate honey tones, tan skin, and large doe-brown eyes, which widened when she spotted my companion. "Rian!"

She trotted over to him with her arms open for an embrace, which he obliged, bending down to give her a firm hug. "Good to see you, Mickey."

"You too!" She drew back, but not before pressing a kiss to his cheek. "How the hell are you?"

Something in me bristled at the scent mark on his cheek. Neither one realized she'd left it, but I knew. And I... didn't like it.

But that was ridiculous. It was a peck on the cheek between friends.

Between more than friends?

Mickey was giving off all the signals that she was attracted to Rian. Her scent had changed, growing warmer and more enticing. That same warmth was reflected in her gaze, and I caught the subtle lick of her lips, how she leaned toward Rian as though caught in his gravity.

I didn't like it.

Why didn't I like it?

Before I could ponder that any further, Rian waved me over. "Mickey, this is Logan Davis. He's a professor at UVic."

Mickey wasted no time holding out a hand for me to shake, which I did. "Always wonderful to meet a friend of Rian's. I was beginning to think he didn't have any."

"Hey!" Rian protested. He looked at me sheepishly. "I have friends."

"You have *brothers*, dude. Not the same thing." She grinned. "They certainly don't look as enthusiastic as this guy does when they walk in here."

I looked enthusiastic? I guessed I felt enthusiastic too, though the emotion was muted, as everything was these days. "Your shop is incredible."

"Thank you." She looked around, wonder and pleasure written all over her face and scent. "Some days it's hard to believe I made this a reality."

"How do you know Rian?" The question slipped out unintentionally. Good goddess, it was none of my business.

"I've been seeing him for years."

The sentence hit me like a fist to the solar plexus. They were together? For years. I swallowed. "Oh."

Rian gazed at me for a second, then gestured at Mickey. "C'mon, Mick. Off with the coat."

I shook my head, utterly confused. "No, that's okay. I—"

But Mickey had already shed her blazer, revealing a full sleeve of tattoos covering her left arm. She held it out for me, and I absently noted that the ink was done in a marine theme, featuring a killer whale, a mermaid, and what appeared to be a ghost ship, among other images. Buried in the patterns, I spotted a familiar symbol. After examining Rian's self-created runes for a short time, I recognized his work.

"Isn't it great?" Mickey swept her other hand over her arm as though she felt a connection to the ink. I supposed she must—it was a permanent part of her. "I love his work so much."

"It's magnificent," I agreed.

She beamed at me as she shrugged back into her jacket. Now that I knew it was there, I caught a glimpse of the ink peeking beyond the cuff of her sleeve. "Thank you. Though my customers don't always appreciate the decoration, so I prefer to keep it covered at work." She rolled her eyes. "It's like they think antique shop owners can only be white-haired, stodgy old men."

Despite myself, my lips twitched. "It's the same in the academic world. So many of my female colleagues get over-looked because they're not white, not men, not old, or missing some other identifier that would make them *serious*."

"What's your area of expertise?"

"Anthropological evaluation of legends and lore of the Middle Ages."

"Oh my god. You are my kind of people!" Before I could react, she latched onto my arm and tugged me deeper into the store. "Come on. I've got some things you're going to love."

I cast a look over my shoulder at Rian as Mickey led me away, but he grinned and shrugged, happy to abandon me to his friend.

My brain spun as we left Curios. The sun had dipped behind the buildings, darkening the street, and there was a chill in the air now that it was denied the warmth of the sun's rays. I'd lost *hours* in the store, something that hadn't happened in ages. Getting caught up in what I was doing like that, letting the fun of something overwhelm me—well, it wasn't me anymore. Except maybe it was. Or it could be, given the right incentive.

Surprisingly, Rian hadn't gotten bored or encouraged me to move along. He'd seemed more than content to watch Mickey and me discuss legends and stories or dream up possibilities for the items we explored in her shop. She knew the provenance for some, but not all, and combining her knowledge with mine was fun. More fun than I'd had in...I couldn't remember when. I had a bag full of trinkets I couldn't leave behind and a heart that felt an iota lighter than it had walking into the place.

Rian paused on the sidewalk in front of Curios, his head tilted to the rapidly deepening sky. When he looked at me a second later, he wore a relaxed smile. "Dinner?"

It was still early, and I wasn't all that hungry, but for some reason, I couldn't say no to him. "Sure."

His smile widened into a full-on grin, and something in my gut poked at me. "Great. I know a perfect spot."

He headed down the sidewalk, and I jogged a few steps to catch up with him and walk by his side. Most of the stores we passed had their OPEN signs flipped to CLOSED. Some were dark and empty, while others still had their interior lights on, showing workers tidying up for the night. The traffic wasn't as heavy as earlier, and most of the cars that had taken up parallel parking spots along the street had disappeared. It was far from quiet—even with a lull in the cars driving along Main Street, I could hear the steady buzz of traffic on adjacent streets. Arrington wasn't asleep for the night. That was for certain.

Suddenly, Rian stopped and eyed me with a worried look. "Do you like Indian?"

"Indian food? Yes. Love it."

His expression eased. "Oh, good. Sometimes I forget that not everyone—"

Movement out of the corner of my eye had me acting before I could even register what I was seeing. My hand shot out to catch the item thrown at Rian. When my palm connected with a smooth surface, I understood what I'd prevented.

I held a lit Molotov cocktail.

Chapter 6

Rian

It took me a second to realize what was in Logan's hand. Then I caught the rough rumble of the motorcycle roaring down the street and put two and two together.

The mountain lion pride was back, and they were out for blood.

Logan yanked the burning cloth out of the bottle of clear liquid, threw it onto the sidewalk, and stomped the fire out. "What the fuck?"

I'm not sure what was more shocking—his decisive action or the F-bomb.

He placed the bottle on the ground, a foot or two away from the charred cloth, then rose and grabbed my arms. "Are you okay?"

"I'm fine," I assured him. A bit dazed by the sudden attack and how Logan had prevented it from being far worse than it was, but unharmed. And, not going to lie, more than a little stunned at how he was running his hands over my arms, checking me for injuries.

"Why would someone do that?" he demanded, his voice

nothing like the burned-out, tired professor I'd known up to this point. Now he sounded like a pissed-off werewolf, growly and intense.

My body was starting to get the wrong idea from his manhandling, so I gently disengaged. "It's a long story. I'll tell you over dinner."

"Over dinner?" Logan's brows rose. "Are you kidding? We need to call the police."

I shook my head and bent down to retrieve the bag he'd dropped when he caught the Molotov cocktail the pride member had lobbed at me. I had a quick look inside, but Mickey had wrapped all of the items in tissue paper. I hoped they'd survived their rough handling. I held the bag out to Logan. "The cops can't do anything. This is a paranormal thing."

"Throwing a weapon at you is certainly *not* a paranormal thing." He took the bag with a gentleness that was totally at odds with the growl in his voice. "Fine. Dinner. But you're telling me everything."

"Deal."

Kerala Sunrise was a hole-in-the-wall restaurant at the end of Main Street, a few blocks from Curios. From the outside, it didn't look like much—the sign over the door was plastic and yellowed with age, and the fonts on it were those I associated with a time in the twentieth century before we'd awakened. The large picture window was draped with heavy orange-and-yellow curtains, swept to either side but still covering much of the glass, and the window bore old, battered posters about the type of food available. It was dark inside, and the furnishings matched the age of the sign, but the scrumptious aromas from the kitchen erased everything else from my mind, as always. It smelled so good here, of warmth and spices and care.

The hostess, who was also one of the owners, recognized me, though we'd never exchanged names. Her English wasn't good, but we got by with smiles and gestures. She held up two fingers, and I nodded, so she grabbed two menus and led us to a small table. It was early for dinner, not quite five-thirty, so there was no one else at any of the other tables. I expected we wouldn't be crowded, even as a more proper dinner hour approached, since much of their business was takeout.

"Spill," Logan ordered as soon as we sat down.

I liked Logan's unassuming professor side, but this more domineering aspect of his personality was also working for me. Too well. "Can we order first?"

He grumbled but turned his attention to the menu. After a second, his brow furrowed. "This is not the type of Indian food I'm used to. What's a parotta?"

"Like naan, but better. I could order for us."

Logan closed his menu and sat back. "Sure. Please."

I had never dated. None of my brothers had because how could we? When anything got hot and heavy, we couldn't hold on to our human forms. It took a special person to understand that and still desire us as gargoyles. We'd found two—Elizabeth and Josh—and that was two more than I thought we'd find. I loved my aunt for trying to give us hope and a way out, but the true-love clause was bullshit. No one was going to want to be with my goblinesque visage.

But if I were to date, Logan would be my type. I couldn't deny it. Calm, big, unassuming, most of the time, with a steel backbone that became obvious when he needed it to be. Like right now. He was happy to let me take the lead in ordering dinner, but I knew that as soon as that was done, he'd be back to ordering me to tell him everything.

It *worked* for me.

Sure enough, as soon as the hostess walked away with our order, he leaned over the table, all intense again. "Is what happened back there part of why you wanted me to come here?"

"Why would you think that?"

"It seems like it might be connected."

I tilted my head back and forth. "Yes and no. I invited you here to find a cure for the curse, and my drive to find it is what I told you—the magic is fading. But that biker...he's a member of a mountain lion pride connected to the Fomori who cursed us."

Logan frowned as he processed that information. "Why?"

I let out a humorless chuckle. "I have no idea. They showed up in Arrington about a month ago and started harassing us. We allied with a wolf pack and tried to drive them out, but that's when the Fomori showed her face. She made a bargain with my parents before Teague was born— she would give them something to help my mother get pregnant, and in return, my parents would pledge their first-born son to be the Fomori's husband when he reached the age of thirty. Except my parents refused, and she poisoned them."

I hadn't shared that level of detail when I'd told Logan about the curse. It was still hard to wrap my head around the Fomori's motivation since we hadn't learned of it until recently. For five hundred years, we'd believed the violence against my parents was random. It was difficult to comprehend that it wasn't. Not that it made it any easier to accept their murders.

"So why would she partner with this pride?"

"That's the question. She's promised them Arrington as

their territory, so their motivation in helping her is clear. But her motivation in using them is what I can't figure out. She poisoned my parents on her own, so she's capable of doing what she feels she needs to do."

"But she got caught," Logan pointed out.

We paused as our food arrived—idiyappam with curry, appam with ishtu, nadan kozhi varuthathu, and, of course, multiple servings of parotta, all served family style. I watched with pleasure as Logan sampled the dishes, hummed appreciatively, and selected more. One of the best things about this new century was being able to try out new culinary experiences right in our own backyard and share them.

"Good?"

He nodded, mouth full.

There was little more satisfying than that.

We ate in silence for a time. I savored every spice exploding on my tongue and tried not to think that this could be the last time I experienced these tastes. No matter if my century-long sleep started tomorrow or two years from now, this restaurant surely wouldn't be in operation when we awoke next. Everything we'd gotten used to would be gone—places, culture, people.

The people would be who I mourned the most, obviously. I also tried not to dwell on the fact that the people I mourned would now include Logan.

When he'd had his fill, Logan leaned back again. "She got caught," he said, continuing our conversation as though we'd never paused to eat. "It makes sense she wouldn't come at you directly, especially now that you've got the advantage of your other form. She needed allies."

"Maybe. But it still doesn't explain why the cats came at us indirectly at first too."

"They were testing you. Learning your reactions to things. A pride isn't the same as a pack—they have the group for convenience and for a place to belong, but they don't work together like werewolves. They're more likely to have a common goal but take independent action."

"That fits with what they've done so far, for sure." I tilted my head and looked at him intently. "You know a lot about prides."

Logan's expression tightened. "I've tangled with mountain lion shifters before."

"That doesn't sound good."

He waved a dismissive hand. "It was a minor territory dispute when I was—a long time ago."

I wondered at the hitch in what he'd said and what he *hadn't* said but didn't press the topic. Instead, I shook my head at the ramifications of the pride being back. "To be honest, we're not sure what to do. If this were back before we were cursed, we'd take it to the king and make our claims under Brehon law. But Brehon law doesn't exist anymore, nor does our king." I gave him a crooked, rueful smile. "We tried taking a more modern approach—attacking them through computers—but the effects lasted less than a month before they regrouped and recovered their courage. And now they've left minor annoyances behind, going right for attempted murder." Not that the Molotov cocktail would have killed me since I would have transformed into my gargoyle form and my stone skin would've been unaffected by the flames. But it could have hurt others. Like Logan.

An image of his clothes and hair on fire took root in my brain, and I shuddered.

Logan's head was turned to the window, but his eyes were distant, not seeing the posters plastered to the glass or the sidewalk beyond. "We need to find their motivation."

"We know that. The Fomori has promised them Arrington as their territory."

He was silent for a moment before turning back to me. "I don't buy it."

"Becker, the pride's leader, said—"

Logan shook his head. "He might have said that, but I don't think it's the truth. Cats go for easy. If it's not easy, they move on."

"Is that what happened in that dispute you mentioned?"

"Yes. They tried to move in on us, we resisted, and they gave up almost immediately. So what you told me fits—that they poked at you and your defenses, tried and failed to take over, and left you alone. What *doesn't* fit is that they would renew their campaign now."

"Unless the Fomori is coercing them somehow."

"Exactly." Logan gave me a grim nod. "That's what we need to find out. How is the Fomori controlling a pride of mountain lion shifters? If we can figure that out, we'll know how to stop them."

"We?"

He tilted his head, his lips twitching in what I now recognized as his version of a smile. "I'm here. I'd be remiss if I ignored this issue completely, wouldn't I?"

It might not have been a firm declaration of friendship, but it was close enough. I held a hand out over the table, and Logan grasped it immediately. "Welcome aboard, Dr. Davis."

Chapter 7

Logan

I'd never been a fan of research assistants, but they were a necessary evil in my line of work—*necessary* being the keyword. My assistant at UVic, Ella, kept my personal library organized, helped me evaluate requests for my expertise, wrote grant applications—basically, she did all the nitty-gritty tasks that would otherwise interfere with my actual work.

But she was always *there*.

Her presence never faded into the background. I could never forget she was there. It wasn't solely an Ella problem —every research assistant I'd ever had posed the same issue. I wasn't sure if it was because they wanted to learn from what I did and therefore scrutinized me when they thought I wasn't paying attention or...I don't know. Maybe my wolf felt threatened by them and refused to let me get into the zone needed to do my research effectively.

Strangely, Rian was no such obstacle.

It didn't make sense. He wasn't trained to be an assistant, and he certainly wasn't trained as a researcher, though it became clear over the next few days that he'd taught himself how to chase down clues hidden in texts, much like I did. Together, we lost hours in companionable silence. I didn't forget about his presence, but for some reason, it didn't bother me. More importantly, it didn't bother my wolf side. There was no itch at the back of my brain to *stay aware, stay on guard*. Even when he insisted we stop for rest or food or to take a break, which would usually have me all but snarling at Ella.

Rian was different. Well, I mean, obviously. But somehow, he *fit* in a way none of my other assistants had.

He pushed back from the table, making room to stretch his arms above his head and lean side to side. He was in his living stone form, wearing a pair of charcoal-gray athletic pants and a worn, faded, shape-hugging T-shirt that bore an unrecognizable logo. His taloned feet were bare, and his horns jutted full and proud from the crown of his head. Over the past few days, I'd gotten used to his red-hued eyes, and my gut no longer clenched at the sight of them.

"My brain keeps going in circles." He rubbed one of his eyes, a gesture that quickly grew into rubbing his entire goblinesque face. "I don't know if I've found something or not."

His voice wasn't as energetic as usual, and a quick glance at the window told me why. Darkness surrounded us. Night had fallen without me noticing—which, let's be real, was not a shock.

I closed the lid on my laptop and leaned onto my forearms, bracing against the table. "Hit me."

He flipped back a few pages in the book he was reading, one of the many he'd transferred from the library in the main house to the guesthouse. About two dozen tomes littered the various surfaces in my temporary home—or more than two dozen, I realized, my eyes sweeping around the great room. Rian had brought over another armful this afternoon.

"It's the story of someone else who made a deal with a Fomóir," he began, falling into the Irish pronunciation as effortlessly as I could drift into Greek. "Aíbinn was a fair maiden who was nonetheless jilted by two lovers. When she saw the beauty of their new wives, she sought out a witch to help her secure a husband. The witch wouldn't help, so she found a member of the Tuatha Dé and demanded their assistance. They also refused her. So Aíbinn found a Fomóir."

"Uh-oh."

Rian shot me a grin. "Indeed. The Fomóir agreed to help her and asked for no price in return—honey, what the hell were you thinking." He shook his head and continued. "They gave her a vial to pour into the village well, which they assured her would diminish the beauty of all the women in the village and 'raise her above all others in the regard of men.'"

"Let me guess. It was poison."

"Bingo. It killed the other women in the village, though not the men, surprisingly, and Aíbinn was quickly identified as the culprit. On the night before her execution, the Fomóir came to visit her. Aíbinn accused them of misleading her. The Fomóir laughed and said Aíbinn had gotten exactly what she asked for—the attention of all of the men in the village." He tapped a taloned finger against the delicate paper. "Thoughts?"

"It could be a morality tale."

"True. Be careful what you wish for, be true and good in your thoughts and intentions sort of thing. But I find it interesting..." His voice trailed off.

After a few moments of silence, I prompted, "What?"

He cleared his throat. "Like I said, I don't know if this is anything."

"Well, spit it out, and let's discuss it." I leaned back, waving one hand for him to get on with it.

He chuckled. "Okay. In this story, the Fomóir uses poison. Our Fomori—" His face contorted for a second, but then he continued on. "She used poison against our parents."

"Fomori may have a thing for poison."

"Right, they could. But here's what's bugging me—she could have cursed us to die."

"Not if she wanted Teague as her husband."

"Fine, not all of us, just the brothers she didn't need. Why didn't she?" Before I could answer the question, he continued, "When she had Josh cornered in Drew's garage, she could have strangled him or kept beating his head into the wall. Instead, she lets him go while he's still breathing and sets the garage on fire. Hell, why use the pride at all? She's powerful enough to come at us directly."

He'd told me the details about their confrontation with the Fomori at Drew's garage earlier, so he didn't need to share more than that small reminder. As I thought it over, realization dawned. "Except maybe she *can't*."

Rian flipped the pen he'd been toying with onto the table. "Exactly."

"So you think she's unable to kill anyone outright." I frowned. "But you could argue that killing someone with poison is the same as killing them with a knife. The poison is a tool."

"But she doesn't need to be present when the poison kills them. Maybe that's enough of a loophole for whatever rules she has to abide by."

"I've never heard or read any legends about the Fomorians with this sort of restriction to their actions. There are plenty of tales about them being in battles with...well, everyone in ancient Ireland and killing without a care."

"Then maybe it's not a Fomorian thing, but a *this* Fomori thing."

"Interesting theory."

"Yeah." Rian retrieved his capped pen and began tapping it against the open book in front of him. I almost told him to stop before he damaged the book, then remembered it was his book. "I don't know if that's something we can exploit to stop her though."

"I'm sure we can." But the *how* wasn't coming to me. My brain felt mushy from hours of reading and researching. Normally, I'd push through and find my second wind, but the lethargy settling into my bones told me there was no second wind to be had. I was tapped out.

"You okay?"

I met his concerned gaze, struck once again by how observant he was. Or maybe I wasn't as good at hiding my bruised and battered psyche as I thought. Or maybe something about this man, this gargoyle, invited me to let down my guard and be open with him. I hadn't had that in so long. I wanted it. More, I think I needed it.

"No." It came out shaky and uncertain, which was odd because it was the truest thing I'd said in ages.

"It's not only tiredness, is it?"

I shook my head.

"And not burnout."

"No."

Rian closed the book after marking the page with a folded paper and stood. "Come on, let's sit down." At my raised brow, because weren't we already sitting, he rolled his eyes and gestured at the part of the great room with the couch and armchairs. "I mean somewhere more comfortable. You want a coffee? A beer?"

He headed toward the kitchen, and I got up to choose a seat on one end of the couch. "A beer, please."

"You got it."

He returned a moment later with a tallboy can of some craft brew I'd never heard of, but I wasn't much of a beer connoisseur. If I was going to talk with him about meaningful and very personal topics, it would be helpful to have something occupying my hands.

Sheepishly, he held out his own can to me. "Could you pop the tab for me? The talons make it difficult."

I took the can, did as he asked, then handed it back.

"Thanks."

He poured a swallow into his mouth. It was an odd way to drink, but then I realized he had to work around the obstacle of his pointed chin. How inconvenient. We sat silently for a handful of minutes, enjoying our beers, and I found it strangely peaceful. I barely knew this man, and yet, his presence was soothing.

"I'm happy to sit here and have some quiet time," he said, his voice a low rumble. "I'm also happy to listen. I'll leave it up to you." He shot me a smile that almost humanized his grotesque countenance, showing me the kindness of the man beneath the monster.

"Growing up," I started, then stopped as my voice hitched. Clearing my throat, I began again. "Growing up, it was my mom, my twin brother, and me. Mom raised us on her own. When we were older, we got the full story on that —she'd gotten pregnant at eighteen by accident after fooling around with an exchange member of the pack."

I saw the question in Rian's eyes and explained, "Packs often do formal exchanges of young members to spread knowledge and, hopefully, diversify the gene pool. Except Mom having sex with this exchange member—who was quite a few years older, in his late twenties, I think—wasn't sanctioned. She was the alpha's daughter, so the wolf, my father, should have approached him for permission to court her. It was all very old-fashioned. Probably still is."

I shook my head at the inanity. "Except my father wanted nothing to do with cubs. He made that very clear to everyone—my mom, my grandfather, and the alpha of his home pack. The alphas were going to force a true mating, which my mother absolutely did *not* want—it's basically tying your soul to another person for life. She didn't want to be tied to a man who wasn't interested in being a father, so she ran away."

"I can't blame her."

"Me neither. Can you imagine? I don't know what the alphas were thinking—that would've been a nightmare all around."

Not for the first time in my life, I took a moment to appreciate my mom's actions. It had to have been frightening as hell, breaking away from her pack and deciding to make her own way in life, but she'd done it for Lyle and me.

"So, yeah, she raised us by herself. She was friendly with the local pack on Vancouver Island, but after her experience with her own pack, she didn't want to join them. So we were, for all intents and purposes, a pack of three. And that was all we needed. Mom, Lyle, and me."

I took a deep swallow of beer to distract myself from how my throat tightened as I thought about speaking aloud this next part. "About six months ago, I noticed Mom had lost a lot of weight. I'd been gone for a month for work, and when I got back, it was so obvious. Lyle hadn't seen the change because he was with her nearly every day, and it had been gradual. I asked the local pack's healer to come see her —that's about as close to a doctor as we can get. They found —" I broke off, overwhelmed with the memory of that horrible day. "They found a tumor in her abdomen, fast-growing and..." I swallowed. "There was nothing we could do about it. She was gone a week later."

A cool hand on my arm brought me out of my memories. Rian had moved closer without me realizing, close enough he could touch me easily. And, oh gods, I hadn't grasped how absolutely touch-starved I was because that simple gesture made my skin light up, burning through the fog that had enveloped my brain and nerves for the past few terrible months.

"I'm so sorry," he said. "I don't know much about were-wolf physiology, but I've heard about a 'wasting disease' that can come on very quickly."

"It's cancer. A werewolf version." I resisted the urge to lean into Rian's comforting touch. He didn't need me all over him simply because he was the first person to show me any meaningful sympathy. My colleagues had expressed their sorrow for what I was going through, but they weren't supernatural creatures—they didn't understand that cancer wasn't supposed to take our loved ones. It was so rare that it did. Why did it have to take my mom?

"Fuck cancer."

That startled a bark of humorless laughter out of me. "Fuck cancer, indeed."

"How did your brother handle it?"

I don't know why I was surprised that Rian asked about Lyle. He had brothers he was close with, so he knew how tight that bond could be. But werewolf twins were a whole other level, one I couldn't begin to express. "Not well. To be fair, I didn't do well either. For a while, it was tough to talk with him because it highlighted that Mom wasn't with us anymore. It took a month or so for us to truly reconnect, and then we leaned hard on each other. We were still dealing with the loss in our own ways, but we knew we were together in it."

Goddess. Until we weren't.

Something in my expression must have clued Rian in to the exponential rise of my inner turmoil. "What happened?"

I gripped the beer can tight enough that the flimsy metal crinkled in protest. "Lyle loved being outdoors. In that way, we're opposites. He pursued forest management as his career, whereas I always had my nose buried in books. He never failed to poke at me about that."

My lips twitched as I remembered how, when we were kids, he would steal my latest read out of my hands and encourage me to come play with him outside instead. "One of the ways he dealt with Mom's passing was by riding his motorcycle. He'd ride for hours to get out of his head. I did the same thing with my research." I swallowed hard. In my mind's eye, I could see the moment I opened the door to the RCMP officer wearing a somber, emotionless expression.

"*Do you know Lyle Davis?*"

"*Yes. He's my brother. What—*"

"*I'm sorry to inform you...*"

"He was driving on a two-lane highway, a route he went on regularly. A semi coming in the opposite direction had a steering wheel tire blowout. It pulled it into Lyle's lane, hitting him head-on." My voice was barely audible. "It was something not even a werewolf could survive."

"Logan..."

The empathy in Rian's voice, the way his hand tightened on my arm—it all conspired to break the blockage in my throat that I'd lived with since Mom died. "In the span of three months, I lost the two most important people in my life. I lost my pack. I lost my family."

Tears flowed down my cheeks, hot and irritating. They were supposed to be cleansing, weren't they? Instead, they annoyed me. I should be stronger than breaking down in front of someone who was a virtual stranger.

Rian took my beer can out of my hands and set it on the coffee table along with his. Then, without a word, he drew me into his arms. "Cry," he said kindly. "Let it out. You're allowed to be sad. You're allowed to mourn. It doesn't mean you're weak. They're gone, and it hurts, and you have to express that somehow."

Five minutes ago, I wouldn't have thought I had been waiting for that permission, but with it, the floodgates truly opened. For the first time since Lyle died, I let myself feel the depths of my grief. And I wept.

Chapter 8

Rian

My heart *ached.*

I knew what it was to lose a parent. A brother. I would never forget waking up to find Odhrán missing, a pile of dust hinting at his fate. And when we woke up this time, it was with the bittersweet knowledge that Finnian had lived his life without us.

But Logan losing his twin so close to losing his mother... I could imagine the devastation that wreaked on his psyche. His entire support system was gone. Not only that but his pack. I would be the first to say I didn't know much about werewolves, but I did know they weren't meant to be alone.

I held Logan as he sobbed, the deep, gut-wrenching sounds bringing tears to my eyes as well. He burrowed into me, indicating how touch-starved he'd been. Had he ever gone months without someone giving him a hug or even a casual touch like I'd seen the MacGrath pack share?

Eventually, the sobs quieted, but Logan made no attempt to disengage. His breathing hitched now and again, the last remnants of the cry fest working their way out of his system. After a few more moments, he said quietly, "I made a mess of your shirt."

"It'll wash."

"You're not as cold as I expected."

"We call this form our living stone form. It's not actually stone—it looks like it, and it's much tougher than our human skin, but not truly stone."

"It's kind of nice. I run hot, so it's refreshing not to feel overheated after a long hug." He pushed away from me and swiped his arm over his eyes. "Thank you. I'm sorry to impose."

"It's no imposition. At all. I wouldn't have offered the hug if I didn't intend for you to take advantage of it. Let me get you a tissue." I got up and retrieved a box from the bathroom, holding out the tissue side to Logan so he could take a few. Then I placed it on the coffee table and returned to my spot on the couch. Well, not the spot I'd originally started out in, the one I'd moved to when he'd started telling his story. I wasn't touching him, but I was close enough that I could, and it was making my insides do funny things.

I'd looked at this man's picture nightly for weeks, imagining who he was and how he could help me and my brothers find a solution to our curse. But in all that time, I hadn't thought of his life beyond his career. Shame rushed through me as I looked at him now, his eyes red and puffy, his nose a matching shade, and his cheeks covered in drying tear tracks. This man had suffered so much in such a short time. The last thing he should be doing was working. Teague had suggested Logan needed a vacation, and I'd agreed, but I didn't realize at the time how right my oldest brother was. The wanker.

"If you were here for fun, what would you do?"

Logan sat back, a fresh tissue in his hand. His expression was puzzled, as though he hadn't contemplated doing something for fun in a long time. Then his lips twitched in what I was coming to recognize as his smile—as much of a smile as he'd let himself have. "Visit a museum."

I laughed. "Of course you would. Why am I not shocked?" Leaning sideways, I bumped his shoulder with mine, then retrieved my phone from the pocket of my athletic pants. Except I couldn't actually use it in this form —my fingers and talons were a threat to the delicate device —and taking on my human skin was difficult at this time of night. I huffed a breath and tossed the useless thing onto the table. "There are a few in Arrington. Do a Google search. We can visit any you like. One or two or...whatever."

Logan frowned. "We should be spending our time researching."

"And we can. But breaks are important."

"I told you I don't need a keeper."

"Oh, a stór, you so do." I immediately cleared my throat. "Uh, that...sorry about that. It slipped out."

"The a stór?"

"Yeah."

"What's it mean?"

Of course he asked. I prayed the dim lighting and my gray skin hid the blush heating my cheeks. "Uh, my treasure."

I waited for him to chastise me for it, but he simply looked at me for a moment, then turned his attention to his phone. It took him seconds to get a Google list of museums in the Arrington area, and he scrolled through. "This one. The Okanagan Indigenous and Natural History Museum."

"Good choice. I've been to that one—their exhibits are awesome." Covering my mouth, I yawned. I didn't need much sleep, but I did need *some*, and it was well into the witching hour. "I'm going to head to bed, but we'll go when we get up, okay? Right after breakfast."

Logan opened his mouth, then closed it, and frowned again, looking away from me.

"What?"

He shook his head. "No. It's dumb."

"Hey. Nothing's dumb." I paused. "Except maybe Teague's jokes. For a guy who can sense emotions, you'd think he'd have a better idea of comedic timing."

Another twitch of Logan's lips. I was getting addicted to that sight. "Would you...stay here? So the house isn't empty when I wake up."

What was that about my heart aching? It nearly *broke* at the tentative request. "Sure. The couch is comfy. I've crashed on it before." Although the guesthouse had two bedrooms, we used one for storage. I wasn't even sure there was a bed under the boxes of things that we'd accumulated over the years.

Relief smoothed out the wrinkles in his brow. "Thank you."

"Don't even worry about it."

It was the least I could do after he'd shared his grief with me. But I would ensure I did much more over the next few days to help ease the burdens on his heart.

WHEN I SWAM up to consciousness the next morning, I realized a couple of things right away. First, I was hot. Too hot. Second, it was hard to breathe. A burst of panic pushed the early morning fuzziness away. Was the house on fire? I flailed a hand and met...fluff.

Blinking my eyes, I immediately discovered the reason

for the heat and the difficulty breathing. A giant wolf was lying on me. He opened one dazzlingly orange eye and let out a long, growly groan. I wasn't sure if it was a noise that meant, *I see you're awake, but I'm not, so don't move* or *don't move, or I'll eat you*. Either way, I decided not moving was the best course of action.

I couldn't quite see all of him from this angle. His head took up most of my field of view. His ebony fur was like silk, though, and I couldn't help sinking my taloned fingers into his ruff. I carefully scratched through his undercoat, scraping my nails faintly against his skin, and he let out another grumbly moan. His eyes didn't open, so I took this particular noise to mean, *yes please, scratches good*. I enjoyed the repetitive motion too. This skin wasn't as sensitive as my human skin, but I could still appreciate the fluffiness of his fur, the sheer thickness of it, and how it flowed through my fingers. Now that I knew that the heat and weight on my chest were from a cuddly wolf and not a house fire, I relaxed into the closeness.

After a few minutes, my eyes drifted closed, and I went off into dreamland once more.

When I next awoke, I was no longer semi-suffocated by a giant wolf. I instantly missed it, which was ridiculous. Yes, he was soft and made fun noises when I petted him, but he was *heavy*. Drawing a full breath was lovely. I hoped he didn't decide he needed more cuddles tonight.

Not that I was planning on staying on the couch again tonight.

I mean, not unless Logan asked me to.

I groaned as I swung my legs to the side of the couch and sat up. At the noise, Logan popped out of the kitchen, looking more refreshed than I'd seen him. There was a good amount of color back in his skin, and he'd taken the time to style his hair and tame his beard. He wore an ice-blue cashmere sweater over a lavender collared shirt paired with charcoal-gray khakis. Nothing bore any signs of wrinkles, and he looked put together. I wasn't naïve enough to think that him unburdening his soul last night—earlier this morning—cured everything, but all signs pointed to him taking steps in the right direction.

"Morning." The corner of his lips tried to form into a smile but failed. Someday I'd see him smile for real, and it would be awesome. "Want a coffee?"

"Please."

He hesitated for a second, then turned and started the Keurig as I stretched my arms over my head and tilted my head from side to side to get it used to the weight of my horns. My spine cracked, letting me know it did not appreciate the couch as a sleeping space.

Logan winced at the noise as he held out the mug of coffee. "That didn't sound good."

"It's fine."

"I, uh." He stopped as I took a sip of the coffee and grimaced. "Oh. It's black. I wasn't sure what you wanted in it."

I smiled. "I need coffee to be aware of how I want my coffee. It's no problem. I know where the cream and sugar are." I aimed for the kitchen to seek out those items.

Logan followed behind. He seemed oddly skittish. He wasn't doing anything as overt as wringing his hands or jumping at my every move, but there was a definite lack of comfort in my presence. It was disappointing. I thought the hug last night had brought us a tiny bit closer together, mentally and emotionally, but maybe I'd misread the whole situation.

Finally, Logan spoke up as I brought my newly sweetened and creamed coffee to my lips. "About last night—"

Here we go. Maybe I could alleviate some of the concerns I reckoned he'd worked himself up about. "Did you want me to stay again tonight? It's no problem. Or we could move you into a room in the main house if you'd like. It's big, but you'll hear Teague or me up overnight, and that might—"

"It didn't bother you?" he asked incredulously.

"Sleeping here last night? No, it was fine. I'm happy to do it if it helps you."

"No, I mean—" He huffed a breath. "My wolf has a mind of his own."

"Oh." I grinned, showing off my teeth. "That."

"Yes, that. I didn't intend to shift but overnight but clearly my wolf had a different idea." He squinted at me. "You could have shoved me off, you know."

"Well, see, I didn't know that. I thought I might get eaten."

His eyes widened. "I would *never*—"

"I'm kidding, I'm kidding." Mostly. "Your fur is like velvet."

He closed his eyes as his cheeks reddened. "Oh goddess."

I sipped my coffee, enjoying his discomfort. It wasn't that I was a sadistic asshole—his blush meant he was *feeling* something. Maybe being embarrassed wasn't the best emotion to start with, but it was an emotion. I'd take it.

He opened his eyes again. "I'm so sorry I—"

"Nope. Not having it. Your wolf needed cuddles, and I was happy to be cuddled. Or be the cuddler. Whichever. Though, if you want me to stay tonight and do the wolf cuddles thing again..." I paused, debating my next sentence, but decided to go for it. "Maybe we could share a bed?"

Logan's blush deepened, reaching up to his ears. For a second, I thought he'd either pass out or run away, but then he cleared his throat. "Yes. Please. I, uh. Please."

"Awesome. So do I get to be the little spoon? Big spoon? Any tips to keep your fur from tickling my nose or getting into my mouth?"

Finally, Logan's lips curved all the way into a smile. It was brief, barely there before it disappeared, but I wanted to crow in victory. Success! He shoved playfully at my shoulder, and I held my coffee mug to the side to avoid spilling it, laughing all the while.

"Shut up," he grumbled in a voice that sounded strangely like the happy, growly moan his wolf had uttered earlier.

"Learn by doing then. Got it." I chuckled and dodged as he tried to shove me again. "Are we still on for the museum?"

Logan looked down at his outfit, then back up at me, one eyebrow arched. "What, did you think I got dressed up for you?"

"Oh. Ouch." I covered my heart and feigned a stagger. "Right where it hurts, man."

"You ass." But he was smiling again. *Smiling.* "Go get dressed."

"Ratty T-shirt and holey jeans okay?"

His eyes narrowed, but all he said was, "Whatever you're most comfortable in. I won't judge."

Uh-huh. Sure he wouldn't. I drained the last of my coffee, put the mug in the sink to deal with later, then gave him a jaunty salute before heading for the door.

Right before I closed it, I was sure I heard him mumble, "That butt would look good in anything."

It took everything in me to keep walking since it was clear he hadn't meant for me to overhear that aside. But I put it in the win column. Two smiles, a blush, a witty bit of banter, *and* a flirty comment?

Hell yes, we were making progress.

Chapter 9

Logan

The Okanagan Indigenous and Natural History Museum was exactly what I needed. The exhibits were perfect in their simplicity and connection to the area around Arrington. The curator loved their work, evidenced by how they included as much local flavor in each description card as possible. The exhibits ranged from Indigenous regalia, on loan from the local First Nation, to the stories of beasts that roamed this land long before people ever did.

For the first few exhibits, I read part of the cards before moving on...at least until Rian noticed. He nudged my shoulder with his. "There's no rush. Read."

So I did.

I loved my brother dearly, but patience had never been his strong suit. Outdoors, yes—he was always very in-tune with his wolf and could employ as much patience as he needed when rambling through the wilderness. Anywhere else in his life? Not so much. Especially not in museums when I wanted to linger over the knowledge imparted by every exhibit. So I'd adopted the habit of skimming the description cards when I was with someone.

But Rian gave me permission to take my time. Absorb. And he didn't make impatient noises or grumble or check his phone—all things Lyle had done. Instead, Rian read each description card too. He pointed out things he saw in the exhibits that were nearly always different from my observations. In short, he was a model companion.

Though I knew I shouldn't be so vain, I was happy about his outfit choice too. If he'd decided to wear an old T-shirt and jeans, I would've lived with it. But instead, he'd turned up in a blue-and-green-checked button-down paired with nice dark-wash jeans, golden-brown Timberland lace-up boots, and a brown leather jacket lined with sherpa fleece to protect against the weather. A dark-blue hooligan hat covered the remnants of his horns. He looked sharp.

And the jeans did amazing things for his butt.

I drew my eyes away from that intriguing part of his anatomy—again—and refocused on the exhibit in front of us. Rian was absorbed in the display of Indigenous tattooing practices. The pictures in this exhibit showed the hand-poked tattoos of the Syilx Okanagan people, as well as the Nlaka'pamux and Ktunaxa. There were a few faded sienna-hued pictures depicting facial and hand tattoos. Next to them were the tools the tattooers would have used—small sticks with sharpened ends. One had a metal needle.

"I find it fascinating that people have been decorating themselves for millennia, and yet the practice is still not fully accepted," Rian said quietly.

I wrinkled my nose. "Well, when someone gets a poop emoji tattoo like the one I saw on Instagram, it's hard to take it seriously."

Rian turned to face me, his expression somber. "But it's

that rush to judgment that's hurtful. You don't know what prompted that choice. Maybe it was a spur-of-the-moment decision they'll come to regret, or maybe it has meaning. It could be a reminder that when life goes to shit, they're still carrying on. It could be a tribute to a loved one who liked that particular emoji, so they chose to permanently etch it into their skin. You don't know."

I hadn't considered it from that perspective, and shame suffused me. I should know better than to leap to judgment. "You're right."

"Tattooing is deeply personal. Even with modern tattoo techniques, you're sitting in a chair or lying on a table for hours, having an artist ink a design permanently into your skin. You're their canvas. You're going to bear their art for your lifetime—unless you go through even more pain and time to have it removed, which doesn't always work perfectly."

"You really love what you do."

He grinned, and I was caught off guard by seeing his human smile instead of his toothy gargoyle one. There was no doubt this smile was far less threatening, with his straight white teeth, pale but rosy lips, and normal mouth shape, but I missed the uniqueness of his goblinesque features.

"I do. It feels like what I was meant for." His eyes sparkled with the admission, and as he continued, he lowered his voice. "The other times I was awake, I focused on sketching and painting. I sold a few pieces here and there solely because we needed the money. When we woke up in 1999, and I saw tattoos everywhere, I was intrigued. I felt drawn to it. So I did an apprenticeship, discovered how amazing it was, and haven't looked back."

The deep passion in his voice was unmistakable, truth ringing in each word. How he felt about tattooing was how I felt—how I used to feel—about my research. Learning new legends and comparing them to those in other cultures had been the driving force in my life for so long. Until it wasn't. I didn't know when it had lost its appeal, or maybe it hadn't, and I'd grown too numb to recognize my passion for anything anymore.

I was so tired of being numb.

"Tattoo me." The words slipped past my lips without thought, but as soon as I said them, I recognized their rightness.

"What—are you serious?" Rian frowned. "Don't get me wrong, I'm flattered, but—"

"Something to commemorate Mom and Lyle with one of your runes for strength or fortitude." I snapped my fingers. "Resilience. I could use an extra dose of that."

"Are you sure?"

I appreciated him asking, but I could hear the thread of excitement in his voice. He *wanted* to tattoo me and probably already had ideas rushing through his creative brain. "I'm sure."

His grin was absolutely *blinding*. "You won't regret it. I promise."

Two hours later, we were at a pizzeria that served wood-fired pizzas Rian swore were amazing. He wasn't wrong. The dough was thick, perfectly crusty on the outside, chewy on the inside, with the exact right amount of toppings. The house sangria paired well with the pizza, bringing out the flavors of each, and after the initial sip of my first glass, I ordered a pitcher.

I was waxing poetic about the museum, rambling on

and on about my favorite exhibits, and Rian wasn't merely smiling and nodding—he was asking questions and offering his opinions. He wasn't humoring me. He was actually interested in what I thought and why and not afraid to share his ideas, even when they contradicted mine. The conversation was surprisingly stimulating, mentally. I hadn't been this challenged in a long time.

"I think the dioramas are one of the best parts of that museum. They give visitors a glimpse into the wilderness they might not otherwise get." Rian punctuated his statement with a bite of his pizza.

"Hard disagree. They're unnecessary. And creepy." I shuddered.

"You didn't like the wolf one."

No. No, I certainly hadn't. My inner wolf had been very distressed at seeing the unmoving, unalive, but snarling creature set behind a pane of glass. "Do you blame me?"

"I suppose not. But still. You have to admit the moose one was impressive."

"Moose, in general, are impressive. A taxidermied one is creepy."

"I kind of wanted to climb up on its back."

I laughed. "And that would be why they're behind glass panels."

He paused and set down his piece of pizza. "That was a good sound."

"What?"

"Your laughter."

I rushed to take a sip of sangria to cool down the burn in my cheeks and fought the urge to apologize, of all things. I didn't need to say sorry for enjoying myself. I didn't need to feel bad about it. I was still alive.

Guilt stole my breath, and I put down my wine glass harder than I meant to.

Rian's expression transformed from appreciative to concerned in an instant. "Are you okay?"

The pizza I'd eaten sat like a block of clay in my stomach, and I pushed my glass away. "I shouldn't be doing this."

"What?"

I swallowed. "Enjoying myself."

Before I could draw back any more, Rian grabbed my hand. I jolted at the sudden touch but quickly relaxed into it. This was one of the things I'd missed most after my mom and brother died—simple human contact.

"Walk me through your thoughts. Because you were so light a moment ago."

"When you said my laugh was a nice sound"—I paused —"my first reaction was to apologize. Then I chastised myself, insisting I have every right to enjoy myself and laugh because I'm still alive."

Rian interlaced our fingers, his thumb rubbing against the heel of my hand. "You're not wrong."

"I know. But it was the *way* I thought it. Like I was directing the statement that I was still alive to Mom and Lyle. That's wrong."

"Is it?" He tilted his head, watching me as I considered his question. "There's always anger buried in grief."

"It's one of the five stages. Denial, anger, bargaining, depression, acceptance."

"See, I didn't know they'd actually categorized it."

"I did a lot of reading after Mom...and then after Lyle. Though I think I jumped right to depression when he died."

"Understandable. So you haven't really dealt with your anger."

"I shouldn't be feeling anger. It wasn't his fault. He

didn't do anything wrong. The semi driver didn't do anything wrong. It was, quite literally, an accident."

"Here you are, thinking emotions are logical." Rian gave me a gentle smile. "He left you right when you needed each other the most. That would make me angry."

"It's not like he wanted to leave me."

"But he still did. Then you had to deal with his death on top of your mom's. Frustrating, right?"

I didn't want to release the affirmative bubbling up in my throat, but after a few seconds, I did. "Yes. Frustrating. Aggravating. Why couldn't he have taken a different route, one with less truck traffic?"

"He had to have known others."

"Of course he did. Others that had better scenery too. But no, he chose that particular highway. Riding around on a...a death cycle."

"You used that term with him before."

"I showed him all the statistics of injury and death of motorcycle riders, even when they were wearing helmets. He laughed at me." I gritted my teeth. "*Laughed.*"

"And then he went and died on his bike like you thought he would."

"Yes! Goddamn him." I banged the table with my free fist, making the cutlery clatter. The noise attracted a few glances from the patrons at other tables, but I barely noticed them. "It's not fair."

"No. Nothing about this, about him, about your mom... none of it is fair." He squeezed my hand, reminding me that he still held it. "But you're allowed to keep living. You *are* alive. Your mom and Lyle aren't, and even though I didn't know them, I'm going to guess they wouldn't want you to stop enjoying life."

I closed my eyes and inhaled deeply, holding the air for

a count of five before releasing it slowly and opening my eyes again. I could picture Mom chiding me gently—then not so gently if I didn't listen. Lyle would smack the back of my skull, telling me to get my head out of my ass. Both of them would be one hundred percent behind me continuing onward.

"No, they wouldn't."

Rian gave my hand another squeeze and let go. "Let me show you something." He turned in his seat to retrieve an item out of his jacket. I wasn't surprised to see it was a small sketch pad—I'd spotted him drawing in it a couple of times at the museum when he'd abandoned me for a few minutes here and there to sit on a bench and get his creativity out. He flipped through a few pages, then handed it to me. "There's that page and a couple of others after it. What do you think?"

The design I was looking at wasn't perfect—it was unrefined, with faint sketch lines intersecting with darker ones—but even so, it rendered me speechless. It was somewhat abstract, but the movement of what it depicted was immediately clear. Two wolves, running side by side, their tails streaming behind them. I spotted runes buried in the lines, woven into the design so expertly I wouldn't have seen them without knowing Rian's penchant for them.

"Resilience and fortitude," he said when I looked at him questioningly. "That's one option. There are two more."

The next was completely different. Again two wolves, in a style that wasn't quite as abstract as the first but far from realistic. They were shown from behind as they sat together, leaning on each other, their tails entwined. A moon rose over them, with the runes etched into its outline.

The third was a departure from the first two. It depicted one wolf, from the side and back, looking over a mountain valley. The wolf was me, something I could tell even in this lightly sketched form. Rian had captured the shape of my ears and nose after only meeting my wolf once, which was pretty amazing. It was drawn in a much more realistic style than the first two. The wolf's fur was delineated, seemingly ruffled by the wind, and—

"This one." I had to grit my teeth against the emotions it provoked.

"It's the two wolves running through the trees that got you."

I had no words left, so I nodded. The symbolism of it was wonderful. The wolves in the valley were subtle, barely there, almost ghosts—but my wolf was watching them. Some might say the pair of wolves in the trees and the position of my wolf should be reversed, with Mom and Lyle watching over me running, but I loved the idea that Mom and Lyle would always be there if I looked for them.

Perfect.

"Let's do it."

Rian's eyes widened. "Now?"

"No time like the present. I mean, if you're up for it."

"Yeah, sure. But you've been drinking, and I don't—"

"Werewolf," I reminded him in a low tone as I stood and started pulling on my jacket. "I could drink three of these pitchers and barely feel anything. Any other excuses?"

Rian chuckled, his grin widening. "None. I'm totally ready for this."

I took a deep breath, inhaling the spices of the pizza, the sweetness of the sangria, the wood smoke from the kitchen, and the tangy warm-stone scent of Rian himself. "Me too."

Chapter 10

Rian

Logan was not, in fact, ready.

He yelled—actually *yelled*—when I drew the first line on his upper arm.

I stopped the needle and straightened, biting back a smile. "Really?"

"That was *not* a little pinch!" His hazel eyes flared orange. Okay, fair. I may have underestimated the pain—it'd been so long since I'd had my upper arms tattooed that I'd forgotten how intense it could be, especially for a first-timer. "More like you were branding me with a—a wood-burner thing."

I shrugged. "Wait 'til we get to the shading."

"Shit." He drew in a deep breath and resettled himself in the chair. "Okay, go."

"You sure?"

"Yes."

"No more yelling?"

"I'll do my best."

"Because it startles the tattoo artist. Like tapping on the glass of an aquarium."

Logan smirked—a whole new type of smile, kind of, and I stored the sardonic expression in the mental box I'd labeled *Awesome Things About Logan Davis.* "Are you saying you're as intelligent as a fish?"

I sucked in my cheeks to make my lips stick out and wiggled them up and down.

He laughed, a bright, almost surprised sound. "You look all badass with your tattoos and horns, but you're really a dork, aren't you?"

"Guilty as charged. Ready?"

He gave a firm, definitive nod. "Ready."

"If you need to take a break, let me know. This isn't all or nothing, okay?"

True to his word, Logan didn't yell again. The repetitive motions of drawing and wiping away blood and ink lulled me into the Zen state I adored, where my focus narrowed to my art and my client. As with every tattoo I did, I was aware that I was causing pain, so part of my focus was on evaluating Logan's reactions. Was he tensing? Was he getting close to his threshold? Thankfully, he slowly settled farther into the chair, his breathing even and calm, telling me he'd found a similar state as me—one where the pain flowed over him, touching but not overwhelming him.

Time ceased to have meaning. It was rare for me to fall so deeply into this meditative state that everything but my client disappeared. Often my thoughts would drift, thinking about what I'd do after work, what I'd have for dinner, how my brothers' days were going, but not this time. My magic rose within me as I etched the start of the first rune into Logan's skin, imbuing it with my intention. *Resilience,* I whispered in my brain. *Give this man the ability to withstand, to bounce back from trauma, to carry on even when he's burdened.*

My fingertips tingled within my nitrile gloves, but the thin material wasn't enough to block my power. It slipped through, rushing into Logan's skin where I held his arm and through the needle. It sank into his soul, changing the heart of who he was in a subtle but undeniable way.

When my magic retreated, its work done for that particular rune, it left behind something I didn't expect. A connection threading us together. It was barely there, but the fact it existed at all was concerning. I straightened and sat back, frowning.

Logan's frown matched mine. "What *is* that?"

I wasn't surprised he could feel it too. "I'm not sure," I admitted. "It hasn't happened before. But the only other supernatural creatures I've tattooed are my brothers."

"And you're already connected to them." He nodded as if that explanation made perfect sense. "It doesn't feel bad."

I poked at the new metaphysical string tying us together. It felt benign enough. Warm, friendly, almost...familial.

His lips twitched. "I think you magically adopted me."

"Believe me, there's nothing brotherly in how I feel about you." It came out almost as a growl, and I reined myself in. "Sorry. I shouldn't have said that. I—I don't know how this happened."

"Hey." The softness in his voice nudged me out of my self-recrimination. He sat up and angled his legs to hang over the side of the chair so he was facing me. "It's okay."

I shook my head. "It shows that I shouldn't be messing around with magic I barely understand."

One of his big, warm hands cupped my biceps. "Rian, it's okay. Whatever this connection is, it's..." The muscles in his throat worked as he swallowed. "It's exactly what I needed."

I met his earnest hazel gaze. "You're sure?"

"It feels almost like a pack bond. Not quite, but close. And...goddess, I hadn't realized how much I needed that." He smiled at me, a wide, heartfelt expression that conveyed the joy I'd accidentally given him. "Thank you. Thank you for caring so much."

There was nothing for it. I had to kiss him.

The silken pliancy of his lips contrasted perfectly with the scratchy bristles of his short beard. For a moment, I reveled in the intimacy of this simple touch, keeping the kiss chaste, encouraged that Logan had neither frozen in shock nor pulled away. Then he moaned, his lips parted, and all thoughts of keeping things simple fled my brain.

The moment our tongues touched was electric. We danced together in a rhythm as old as time, our tongues ebbing and flowing together as we chased each other's tastes. The accidental connection I'd forged flared to life, gaining strength, and I could feel his soul drink it in. I accepted the truth of what he'd said—that he'd needed that tie. Wanted it.

But did he need or want it with me? Or would anyone have done?

That thought sobered the nearly drunken desire swirling through me. I pulled back slowly and rested my forehead against his.

"I didn't intend for that to happen," I whispered.

"I'm okay that it did." He let out a delicate breath. "But I don't know if I'm...if I'm whole enough for..." He gestured vaguely between us.

"I understand." Making sure he was steady on the chair, I turned back to my cart, pulled off my gloves, and selected a new pair.

"I'm not saying no."

I paused in donning the new gloves, hope surging in my chest. Ruthlessly, I tamped it down, unwilling to pressure Logan. He deserved all the time in the world to recover from his grief and discover who he was on the other side of it.

"You could," I ensured him. "I truly would understand."

"I know you would. You've been nothing but kind and supportive to someone who's a virtual stranger."

The nitrile snapped into place. "I have a confession."

"Uh-oh. What?"

"I, uh." I cleared my throat and cast a sideways glance at him. "I might have stared at your bio picture on the UVic website for a few weeks before I got up the courage to email you."

"Really?" His voice, his laughter, was delighted. "My last assistant took that picture. I convinced her she would make a better photographer than researcher, and she took my advice."

"You're not upset that I virtually stalked you?"

"You didn't harass me. I'd hardly call it stalking." His joy dimmed. "I'm big and fat. For someone like you to want to kiss me—"

"Hey. No. The size and shape of your body have nothing to do with your worth. And for the record, I love how you look. I love that you're bigger than I am. I love the cushiness around your middle. How boring would it be if everyone was the same height, had the same musculature, the same 'in-fashion' hairstyle, and so on?"

Logan stared at me for a moment, his expression all but unreadable. Then he shook his head. "You're amazing, Rian O'Reilly."

"Back at you, Professor Logan Davis." I shot him a grin. "Ready to keep going on those lines?"

THERE WAS an awkward moment when we returned to the guesthouse as we both remembered my promise to stay over again...but this time in Logan's bed. It'd been a platonic thought in the morning sun before we'd shared a wonderful day and an even more wonderful kiss, but now I was feeling anything but platonic toward Logan. And he'd made it clear he wasn't quite ready for things to progress.

I looked at him, and he looked at me—and then solved the problem by stripping off his shirt, shucking off his pants and underwear, and shifting into his wolf. I hardly had time to glimpse his perfect, naked butt before it was replaced by a large, fuzzy wolf's tail.

Then all I could think about was how beautiful he was.

He had black fur all over, a distinct contrast to his naturally dark-blond hair. There were dashes of silver in his tail and at the apex of his ears, but otherwise, all you'd see of him in a nighttime forest would be his bright-orange eyes. His head was level with my chest, which I thought was bigger than usual for a wolf, even a werewolf, but I could have been wrong. I hadn't been around shifted wolves very much, and certainly not close enough to get an accurate idea of their size compared to my own.

He shot me a look over his shoulder and, before I could get my tangled tongue to work, trotted up the stairs to the bedroom.

Then I had a thought. "You'd better not have messed up the tattoo!"

I followed the sound of chuffing to the main bedroom and entered the room in time to see Logan jump onto the bed, turn around three times—which made me grin—and lie down with his thick tail covering his nose. His orange eyes and alert ears tracked my movements as it was my turn to strip. I left my boxers on but tossed the rest of my clothes on the chair next to the dresser. My hat was the last to go, exposing the nubs of the horns I'd taken care to shave off this morning.

It took little more than a breath to release my human skin. Slipping into living stone was familiar, if not welcome. Everything about my body in this form was exaggerated— my facial features and the horns were the worst of it, but my arms were that much bigger, as were my chest, legs, hands, and feet. This form never felt like *me*.

It was exhausting having to return to it constantly.

I tilted my head back and forth, getting used to the weight of my horns again, then climbed into bed, happy to let a pillow take over the work of holding them. I lay on my side, facing Logan, and smiled.

"So, no spooning?"

In response, he propped his head on my bent knees.

Yeah, that would do. I watched him close his eyes, seemingly content, and I did the same.

Chapter 11

Logan

I found myself smiling at the bacon sizzling in the pan in front of me. Who did that? Someone who had apparently rediscovered their ability to fully smile, that was who. I shook my head at my thoughts, but it didn't dislodge the expression on my face.

Yesterday had been...good. Really good. The trip to the museum had been wonderful, as had the meaningful conversations I'd shared with Rian. Then there had been the tattoo, the connection...and the kiss.

It had mirrored Rian himself—at first mild and encouraging but growing deeper as his passion had come through, matching my own. I touched my lips as they tingled with the memory, then chuckled at my fancy. My libido hadn't quite made it back online, but a low buzz in my gut said it could happen with this man. Even before Mom passed, I'd never been one for casual hookups, so after she, and then Lyle, was gone, that part of my life had withered and, I'd thought, died. But apparently, it had gone into hibernation with the rest of my emotions.

Now they were all waking up, thanks to the man who was still fast asleep in my bed upstairs.

Opening my eyes to see a gargoyle in bed next to me should have been frightening, but his features had already become familiar. His scent had wrapped around me like an embrace: warm stone and a slight acridness that whispered *magic* to my senses. I'd still been in my wolf form, and the urge to scoot closer to him had been almost undeniable. But he'd looked so peaceful in his sleep, his expression relaxed, his breathing even, that I decided to get up and make breakfast instead. The least he deserved was breakfast in bed. So I shifted and headed downstairs, eager to show him how much I appreciated him.

It took me a few minutes to find a tray and arrange the plate of eggs, bacon, and sliced tomatoes, the mug of coffee, and the glass of orange juice. I kept my eyes on the tray as I walked upstairs, making sure nothing tipped, and nudged the partially open bedroom door with my foot. It swung wide, and I stepped into the room.

"Wakey wakey, eggs and bac-y," I said in a sing-song voice, knowing the silliness would make Rian smile.

There was no movement from the bed.

"Rian?" I walked a few steps closer. My feet weren't silent—I was too big to be stealthy. But there wasn't so much as a twitch from him.

Was he even breathing?

The items on the tray rattled as my arms suddenly lost strength. I stowed the tray on the nightstand, my eyes never leaving Rian's still—too-still—form. He couldn't be... No. I refused to believe it. He wasn't dead. He was...a sound sleeper.

My index and middle finger sought out the pulse point in his neck, but I couldn't find it. That was better than thinking there wasn't a pulse to find. Fighting the panic that wanted to overwhelm me, I held a trembling hand a centimeter above his mouth and nose.

There. A soft breath.

"Oh, thank the goddess," I whispered. Emboldened, I pushed Rian's shoulder gingerly, then with more force when his body barely moved. "Rian, wake up." Panic threatened to choke me again when there was absolutely no reaction from the gargoyle. I grabbed his shoulder with both hands and put all my strength into shaking him. "Rian!"

Nothing.

I stopped and staggered back a step. This...this is what Rian warned me about. His time running out early and dropping him into sleep for a hundred years. My throat closed up, and suddenly I could barely breathe. This couldn't be happening *now*. We were still researching, still looking for a way out for him and Teague.

I couldn't be losing someone else I cared about.

I couldn't.

Turning tail, I raced out of the bedroom and down the stairs. As much as my wolf wanted out, I held on to my human form, so I'd have hands to open doors. I needed to get help, and thankfully, that was a few steps away.

I hoped.

MY PANIC WAS SOMEWHAT justified when Drew and Josh ran back to the guesthouse with me. The three of us scrambled up the stairs, Drew in the lead. The fantasy I'd held on to—that we'd arrive to discover he'd gotten up and started in on the breakfast I'd left—dissipated into nothingness as I spotted Rian in the same position on the bed.

I hesitated at the doorway as Drew reached the side of the bed. Tension suddenly left him, his head and shoulders falling. "He's still in living stone. Thank all the gods."

Josh reached over to rub his partner's back, but I didn't understand the relief. Rian wasn't *waking up*. "How is that good?" I demanded.

Josh glanced over his shoulder and offered me a wan smile. "It means the curse hasn't kicked in. This is one of his 'naps.'"

Oh. I heaved in a breath that felt like the first I'd taken since I found Rian lying motionless. "So he'll wake up."

"Eventually." Drew brushed a hand across his brother's forehead, then leaned down to press a kiss to his stone skin. He straightened and took in the laden tray. "Breakfast in bed, huh?"

Heat flooded my cheeks. "It's not what it looks like."

"It'd be okay if it was." He gave me a genuine smile, though it didn't quite banish the sadness in his eyes or scent. "Everyone deserves to find happiness when and where they can."

He wasn't wrong, but something in my gut twinged at the thought. *Did* I deserve to find happiness with Mom and Lyle gone? My logical side knew they wouldn't want me to be alone forever, an idea Rian had reinforced the night before, but the emotional side of me wasn't convinced for so many reasons. I needed to parse them out but now wasn't the time or place.

"So what do we do?"

Drew shrugged one shoulder as though a giant weight was resting on it. "Nothing. We have to let it take its course. We've tried waking him before, and it didn't work."

I hated everything about this. "And how long...?"

"It varies," Josh said, his voice muted. "Sometimes it's a

few hours, sometimes days. The longest was three days." The drawn look on his face illustrated it had been a hellishly long three days.

Three days. All right. That wasn't forever. I could handle three days. I'd throw myself into research so we didn't lose time. Focusing on my work was my tried-and-true method for making the rest of the world disappear. This situation was no different.

Three days.

On the morning of the third day, I woke in my wolf form on the bed, expecting to find Rian's red eyes open to meet my relieved gaze.

It didn't happen.

He was as still and unmoving as he'd been since that first morning. Breathing shallowly, but breathing. Skin cooler than mine, but that was normal too. There was no sign, none at all, that his nap would end today. Or tomorrow, or the day after.

Maybe Drew was wrong. Maybe his brother wouldn't wake up this time at all.

I wanted to howl from the unfairness of it. Why was this happening right after Rian and I had connected? Was this karma for some wrong I'd done in a past life? Was it punishment for daring to think I could move on without Mom and Lyle?

A whine escaped me as I lay with my long snout between my paws. Instinct prompted me to scoot forward to sniff Rian's cheek—he smelled of warm stone and magic, as always—and my tongue darted out, partially for a taste of him and partially to see if the lick would encourage some response. Of course, it didn't. My wolf wanted to nudge him harder, lick more forcefully, but I reined in that impulse. It wouldn't help.

We need to detach ourselves. My wolf whined again at the thought, but human logic wasn't his strong suit. All he knew was that a person we'd both grown to like, who'd selflessly given us a sense of pack we hadn't had in so long—that person was out of our reach, and he didn't like it. My human side knew we needed to put distance between us so it wouldn't hurt as much when he left permanently.

Too late. That thought originated from my wolf side, proving that maybe he was smarter than me. Because as soon as the thought formed, I realized he was right. It was far too late to protect myself.

A knock at the front door prompted me to shift back into human form and pull on whatever clothes I'd abandoned on the floor the night before. When I reached the bottom floor, I wasn't surprised to see Josh's face in the window. The first words out of his mouth when I opened the door weren't a shock either.

"Any change?"

I pulled the door wide and gestured for him to come inside as I shook my head. "Nothing."

"Damn." Josh glanced at the stairs, clearly wanting to see Rian for himself, but he didn't ask, and I didn't offer. No change meant no change, and him going into my room—my temporary sanctuary where *I* kept watch over Rian—to gawk at the sleeping gargoyle wouldn't help the situation.

I expected Josh to take his leave with that news, but he stood on the small rug in the foyer like he had something else to say. Except he wasn't saying it. I let out a sigh. "You want a coffee or something?"

He bounced onto the balls of his feet. "Actually, I was

hoping to entice you out of the house for a little bit." He frowned. "Well, no. Plan A was checking on Rian and celebrating him being awake. Plan B was getting you out of the house if he wasn't. You in?"

I looked at the mess of my research on the dining room table, my laptop swimming between sheets of paper with my chicken-scratch writing that even I could barely read. I'd been going around in circles, unable to truly drown myself in my work, and the thought of getting back to it made me want to shift into my wolf and curl up in bed with Rian's still form.

That was a dangerous route. I'd almost gone down it when Lyle died—taking on my wolf form and staying in it. That was the main reason I hadn't shifted for months.

Everything was simpler when I was in fur. My grief and sadness were still there but of lesser importance than surviving. The emotions couldn't overwhelm me like they did when I wore my human skin. But the longer I stayed in wolf form, the less I saw a reason to return to my human one, and therein lay the danger. I wasn't only wolf and I wasn't only man—I was both, and I needed to acknowledge both.

"Sure. I'm in." Whatever Josh had planned, it would be a distraction, and that was something I sorely needed.

It was eight in the morning, so I was surprised when Josh pulled up to a strip mall across town from the gargoyles' mansion and parked in front of a shop with a sign reading *Moon and Stars Spa*. I wasn't a regular spa-goer, but even I knew spas didn't open until later in the day.

At my dubious look, Josh shot me a grin. "We're good. I know Em and Haider—Em's my bestie. They always make time for me before opening, and when I asked if they could fit you in, they told me I was silly and to get our butts over here."

The corner of my lips twitched, no doubt as Josh intended, and I followed him out of the car.

The interior of the Moon and Stars Spa was not what I expected from the rather plain outside. Inside, it was lush with velvety fabric chairs in the waiting area, draped sheer fabric that gave the space a more intimate feel, and rich, deep colors everywhere I looked—deep indigo, dark eggplant, and crimson—with bronze accents. It could have been overwhelming, but instead, I found some of the tension in my shoulders falling away.

Two humans emerged from the back room, both with bronze skin and sharing enough similarities in their features that I assumed this was the sister and brother who ran the spa, Em and Haider Saqqaf. Josh had given me a brief rundown on who they were on the way over, warning that while Em knew about the supernatural, Haider did not. I appreciated the heads-up.

Em had navy-blue hair draped over her shoulders, and she wore dark skinny jeans with artistic rips across the thighs, a chunky-knit black sweater, and black combat boots with sparkles. In contrast, Haider sported pale-pink chinos and a pastel yellow-to-orange ombre button-down under an off-white sweater vest. His hair was black, shaved on the sides and the back, but long on top and styled immaculately. The siblings were about the same height, an inch or two short of six feet.

Haider stepped up and eyed my height appreciatively. "Look at *you*, Mr. Daddy Bear."

Heat rushed to my cheeks.

Em smacked her brother's shoulder. "That's not how you introduce yourself, you menace."

Haider stuck out his hand, grinning and not at all cowed by his sister's reprimand. "Haider Saqqaf."

I took his hand. "Logan Davis."

"Logan Davis," he purred, still holding my hand. "It looks like you could use my services."

"Haider…" Josh's voice held a note of exasperation.

"Oh my god, Josh. My *aesthetic* services. What did you think I meant?" Haider winked at me. "He's got a dirty mind."

"I do not."

"He doth protest too much."

"Em," Josh said. "Help."

Ignoring Josh, Haider looked up at me with more than lascivious interest this time. "Your skin isn't as vibrant as it should be, and your eyes…" His moue said it all. "Have you been drinking enough water, getting enough sleep?"

"No and no," I answered.

"Honesty! What a concept." Haider looped his arm through my elbow and tugged me away from the hair styling area of the spa. "Come with me and let me have my way with you."

I looked over my shoulder at Josh, but he waved me on my way. "He's harmless. If his flirting makes you uncomfortable, tell him—he'll stop."

"Definitely. It's only fun if the other person appreciates it too," Haider confirmed. "But it *is* fun, isn't it? I think you could use some fun."

He wasn't wrong. Even if I knew the words were empty flattery, it still felt good to be praised. "Flirt away."

"Excellent!" There was a bounce in his step as he pulled

me through an archway. To one side, there was a table and a chair next to a recliner with a bowl where someone's feet would be. To the other, there was a room with a closed door, one Haider quickly opened to reveal a single bed with what looked like a heavy comforter. He adjusted the lights so they were dim for human eyes, but they left plenty of light for me to see. Muted, chill music with flutes and nature noises played in the background, and there was a faint scent of lavender, chamomile, and cedar. It was reminiscent of being in the woods, and it relaxed my wolf more than I thought it would.

"We'll do a facial first," Haider said, pulling back the cover on the bed. "Tame those brows too. Then a mani-pedi, and then we'll let Em tackle your hair and beard."

"That sounds like a lot." Not that I couldn't afford it, but I'd thought we'd be gone for an hour at most. This would dig into my research time far more than I wanted. And what about Rian? What if he woke up while I was getting pampered? How rude would that be?

"Don't worry. You're getting the Josh special. He and Em have been friends for-ev-er." Haider grinned as he drew out the word. "Or since college, which, you know, same thing. Go ahead and take off your shirt...or whatever you're comfortable removing," he amended with a waggling brow. "I'll be back in a few minutes."

Before I could protest about the time this would take, he was out the door, closing it gently behind him, and I was left standing in a room that could be in the middle of the forest if I closed my eyes and ignored the four walls around me. The urge to return to the guesthouse was strong, but I inhaled a deep breath and let it out slowly. Both Josh and Haider were right—I needed a distraction, and I needed to take better care of myself. If that meant a few hours of pampering, then it meant a few hours of pampering.

THE NEGATIVITY that had dogged my thoughts for half a year faded under Haider's soothing ministrations and attention. For all his exaggerated winks and overt flirting, I got the impression he was a true caretaker, keen on making sure his clients felt better when they left than when they arrived. That was certainly the case with me. My face was silky smooth, my hands and feet felt refreshed, and Em finished the experience with a great beard trim and haircut. Of course, getting pampered didn't solve any of the issues facing me, but somehow it lightened my soul.

"I still don't think they charged me enough."

Josh glanced at me, turning his gaze from the mostly empty two-lane highway for a couple of seconds. "They charged you what they charge me—materials only."

"But I'm no one to them." While I appreciated their generosity, it didn't sit well with me.

"You're my friend, so you're their friend." Josh shrugged as he looked in the rearview mirror, then stiffened. "Shit. Not this again."

That's when I picked up the sound of a pair of motorcycles coming up on us quickly. I looked out the back window and confirmed that two riders were suddenly tailgating us. One wore a helmet, and one didn't—his dirty-blond hair was pulled away from the sides and billowed behind him like a ratty flag in the wind. He wore a bandana over the lower half of his face with the illustration of a grinning skull.

"Are they from the mountain lion pride?"

"Yeah. The one without a helmet is Becker, the asshole who leads them." The sour smell of fear wafted up from Josh. "Call Teague."

For a second, I thought Josh was talking to me, but then I realized he'd triggered the hands-free calling on his phone. It rang a couple of times before the call connected, and Josh didn't even let Teague get a word out before he said, "Becker's on my tail."

"Where are you?" Teague's voice came across the line clipped and almost harsh, his professional cop tone.

"Around the same place they ran me off the road last time."

"Wait—they've run you off the road before?" No wonder Josh's knuckles were white around the steering wheel. "Not happening this time. Pull over."

"Is that Logan?"

"Yes, it's me."

"Pulling over isn't a good idea. Keep your speed steady, Josh. I'm on the way."

"Keep my speed steady," Josh muttered as Teague hung up. "Like that's easy when—shit!"

He swerved to the right as Becker came up on the driver's side and slapped a gloved hand against the window. The passenger side wheels hit the unpaved shoulder and there was a tense second when I thought Josh was going to overcorrect to get us back on the road properly. Instead, he guided us back onto the asphalt carefully, the increased aroma of fear belying his outwardly calm appearance.

"I am *not* wrecking another car because of these assholes," he said through gritted teeth.

"Pull over," I ordered.

"But Teague said—"

"I know. But I'd rather face these guys stopped than at eighty k. You?"

Josh grunted but slowed his speed. "I'd rather not face them at all."

"Fair." I unbuckled my seatbelt as he pulled onto the shoulder and stopped. The bikes halted a few dozen meters behind us, their riders likely wondering what the hell we were doing. I wished I knew, but I was operating on instinct. "Here's how we'll play it. We're going to stay in the car as long as possible and wait for Teague to get here. If necessary, *I'll* get out and confront them. *You* stay in the car, no matter what."

"I wish these fuckers would leave us alone," Josh said, his eyes on the rearview mirror.

I turned in my seat to watch the pair of bikers. They seemed to be trying to determine why we'd stopped and were keeping their distance for the moment. "The Fomori's got something on them. Or has something they want. Otherwise, why would they work with her? Mountain lion shifters are notoriously independent."

Josh whipped his gaze to me, eyes wide. "I saw her force a shift on one of them."

"Really?"

"I mean, I assume it was her." He explained how, shortly after this all started and before they knew of the Fomori's involvement, he'd seen one of the pride members in a partially shifted state, with his hands as furry paws. He'd followed the biker to a swanky mansion and witnessed him being expelled from the gate and forced into his mountain lion form. "At the time, we thought it was the alpha's mate or something, but it makes sense that it was the Fomori."

"Has she bound them to herself, somehow?"

"What do you mean?"

I shook my head. "I'm not sure. There are plenty of tales of people making deals with the fae and not ensuring the wording was perfect. The fae—and the Fomori—are master loophole finders. What if Becker had an agreement with her, and she manipulated it, taking control of his pride?"

"It would explain why they haven't given up yet." Josh glanced in the mirror again and tensed. "Shit. They're off the bikes."

Becker and his crony stood in front of their rides, looking as though they were still debating what to do now that we'd stopped. No other vehicles were around. Everything was quiet except for the purring of the car's engine. It took me a second to decide on my course of action. "Stay here."

"You said you were only getting out if it was necessary."

My lips twitched. "It's necessary."

The brisk December air bit at my nose and cheeks as I emerged from the car. The slight breeze couldn't cut through my sherpa-lined jacket, but it was chilly against the newly shorn sides and back of my head. I strode to the back of the car and stopped a few meters away from the trunk, facing the mountain lions, with a good dozen or so meters between us.

"You're new," Becker called over the distance after pulling his face mask down.

I acknowledged that with a tip of my head. "Logan. I hear you're Becker, the leader of the Fomori's pride."

He stiffened at that insinuation. "I'm the leader of *my* pride."

"Except she's the one calling the shots."

I didn't think it was possible, but his shoulders grew even more rigid. "What's your point?"

"Aren't you tired of being a pawn?"

Suddenly he grinned. "Oh, I see. You think you can turn me against her." He wagged a finger at me. "Nice try, Logan. It won't work, but nice try."

"She's got something on you and your pride. You made a deal with her, didn't you? Something that backfired. I can help you find a way out."

His grin didn't fall away, but his eyes tightened. "That's assuming I want a way out."

"You'd rather be tied to her forever?" I tilted my head. "Come on, you're not that stupid. You wouldn't be the leader of the pride if you were. You've got to know that whatever loophole she's got you wrapped around, you're not getting out of it, even if you complete your end of the bargain. Why would she ever willingly let a tool like a mountain lion pride go?"

Becker's crony looked at his boss, worry slashed across his features. "Is that true?"

"He's full of shit," Becker said, glancing at his partner. "This agreement with her is temporary. You know that. Don't start believing what he's spouting off. He doesn't know anything."

"I do though. I'm a professor at UVic, and I study this stuff for a living." I took a step forward, focusing on the crony. "You're right to question it. I'm guessing your boss has made a deal he can never fulfill, and he knows it. But he doesn't want *you* to know."

"Shut up," Becker snarled.

"See? He's not denying it." I took another step forward. "Ask him. Question it—"

"I said shut up!" Becker advanced, his fists clenched at his sides.

I towered over him, but I didn't think he noticed with how angry he was. "And if I don't? Are you going to shift and fight me?" Adrenaline spiked through my system as I leveled my challenge. I tore off my jacket, letting it fall to the ground. "C'mon, Becker. Let's go. Your cat against my wolf."

It took a few seconds for me to shift into my wolf and kick off the remains of my clothes. My blood raced, hot and eager. I wasn't bluffing Becker—I *was* ready for a fight. But the side of me that could still think logically suspected there wouldn't be one, no matter how much I snapped at Becker and his crony, taunting them.

They wouldn't shift. If I was right, they *couldn't*.

We all caught the wail of a siren at the same time. The cats darted back to their bikes. I remained where I was, my teeth still bared in a snarl. Becker paused long enough to hiss at me, and then they were off, racing away from the cops.

Good riddance.

My snarl fell away, but I was still too worked up to shift back to my human form. My wolf wasn't happy that we weren't chasing after our prey. He was also worried about protecting Josh, who was almost-pack. I indulged in a full-body shake as Teague's patrol car approached, knowing he'd give me the time to calm down and watch over Josh while I did so.

But the cruiser that stopped didn't have Teague behind the wheel.

Oh shit.

As if this situation couldn't get any worse, Josh popped his door open. My human mind shouted at me to run into the forest next to the highway, but my wolf was still primed to fight, protect, *save*, and there was no way he'd leave an almost-pack member behind.

"Sir! Stay in your vehicle!" The cop's voice sounded almost frantic over the loudspeaker.

"He's my dog!" Josh shouted. "He's friendly!"

The cop exited his car and focused on me with his gun drawn. "Sir, that's the biggest wolf I've ever seen."

"He's, uh, part Mastiff. Tibetan Mastiff." Josh took a step toward the back of his car. Getting closer to me to indicate I wasn't a threat, my human mind understood.

But all my wolf saw was that our almost-pack member was getting closer to danger.

I bared my teeth and growled.

"Sir! Get back!" The cop jolted around his door while Josh ignored him and took another step. I snarled, ready to protect—

There was a loud *bang* followed by searing heat in my right shoulder.

I staggered, overwhelmed by pain, by the shouting, by everything.

The one thing that came through was Josh screaming, "Run!"

Logic finally took over. If I didn't run, I would be dead, and then how would I protect my almost-pack?

I turned tail and raced into the forest on three legs.

Chapter 12

Rian

The first thing I saw when I woke up was Teague sitting in a chair beside the bed in his gargoyle form. As much as I loved my brother and loved seeing him, I couldn't figure out why he was in Logan's bedroom. At least, not at first. As the fog of sleep lifted and the stiffness in my joints and muscles became apparent as I tried to sit up, I realized what had happened.

Another "nap."

"How long?" My voice was raspy, barely there.

Teague handed me a water bottle. "Today's the fifth day."

"Shite." I downed about a third of the water and forced myself to stop, even though I could drink the rest of it and probably another five. "That's the longest yet."

"It is." His purple eyes watched me intensely. It was tough to read emotions on our faces in our living stone forms, but I'd had centuries of practice. My brother was worried about something. Me, no doubt. But there was something else there too.

I shifted my position to sit on the edge of the bed, my taloned toes on the hardwood floor. "What is it?"

"Logan's missing."

It took me a second to process what he'd said because in no realm did that make any sense. "Missing? Since when? How?"

I would've shot to my feet, but Teague leaned forward and pressed a hand to my shoulder, keeping me seated. "Take it easy. This is the longest you've been out, so you can't—"

I shoved his hand off me. "I don't care about me, you scut. I want to know why you're not out there looking for Logan!"

"Drew and Josh are. So is the MacGrath pack. I came back here because I felt you waking up. Your emotions were resurfacing. I didn't want you to wake up alone."

That mollified me somewhat. "Thank you." I inhaled and let it out slowly, then took another few sips of water. "What happened? Was it the pride?"

"In a way." Teague explained how Josh and Logan had run into the pride on the way home from a spa day—which gave me pause since I hadn't thought that was something Logan was interested in, but the fact Josh had even thought to arrange it gave me warm and fuzzy feelings for my soon-to-be brother-in-law. Logan had confronted Becker on the side of the road, shifted into his wolf form to fight him, but a cop had scared them off. "Josh had called me for help, so they thought the approaching cruiser was me, but it wasn't. Tran was closer, so he took the call. When he approached, all he saw was an enormous wolf threatening Josh, so he shot him."

"He *shot* Logan?"

Teague's hand pressed me down again. "Logan ran off into the woods. He's a werewolf, Rian—they heal fast."

"You don't know that. He could be more injured than you know."

"The pack would've found him if that were the case. They've been able to track him, but he's actively hiding from them."

Okay. That was...not good, but it did indicate he was mobile and thinking. "Why wouldn't he stay put for them to find him?"

"Christopher thinks it's because he doesn't know them, and he's on their territory, injured, so he can't fight. Better to avoid a confrontation."

"I need to get out there." I threw Teague's hand off again and shoved to my feet. My muscles protested, and the room swayed, but everything settled after a second or two.

"You're not in any shape to go traipsing through the woods," Teague said, standing as well.

"I won't need to." I hoped. I made quick work of my long-neglected needs in the bathroom, then continued our conversation when I emerged as if there hadn't been a break. "I tattooed him on that last night. I've got a connection to him. I'll be able to find him, or I'll be able to call him to me. I think, anyway."

Teague hovered at my side as I headed out of the bedroom and down the stairs. "Try calling him to you first, okay? If it doesn't work, I'll take you to where he got shot, and we can try tracking him."

I agreed with that approach, as much as I didn't want to. My legs felt like jelly from simply walking down the stairs. From experience, I knew I wouldn't feel out of sorts for long, but Teague was right—at this moment, I wasn't capable of roaming through the woods.

Though if I needed to so I could find Logan, I would.

Teague set me up in the gazebo near the edge of our yard on a camp chair with more bottles of water and a platter of food Josh had prepared for me that morning. Apparently, he'd done so every day, and when I didn't wake up, the three of them had taken care of it. It had meat, cheese, fruit, and crackers and was the perfect solution to my growling stomach.

Teague's purple eyes glowed in the dim light under the gazebo's roof. It wasn't much better beyond the small structure—the day was gray and gloomy, with precipitation threatening. I hoped Logan made it home before the rain started.

"You good?"

"I'm good," I assured him. My cell phone was next to the platter of goodies on the gazebo's small wooden table. I couldn't use it in my living stone form, but I could shift if I needed to. "You don't have to babysit me."

He grabbed one of my horns and waggled my head back and forth. "I kind of do, baby brother."

I waved a hand, whacking his away from my horn. "Go on, then."

"You'll call if you need anything?"

"Absolutely."

"And if Logan shows up?"

"Of course. Also, if he doesn't." My grin faded. "You need to be out there searching in case this doesn't work."

"I'll call if we find anything."

"Good luck."

"You too."

Teague disappeared into the house, presumably to shift into his human form and get dressed in something more suitable for being out and about than the athletic shorts he'd been wearing as a gargoyle. A few minutes later, I heard his car start up and leave the property, the engine's sound fading quickly.

Then it was just me and the forest.

The woods were quiet, but they were never truly silent. Tree branches rustled together in the breeze. Something small scurried through the underbrush and leaves that had fallen from the few deciduous trees, making the dried foliage crinkle and crack. In the distance, something fell with a subdued crash—a weakened branch, maybe, or an overconfident squirrel.

I spent a few moments listening to the forest while working through Josh's platter and another two bottles of water. It was amazing how eating and drinking made me feel so much better, as though I were reminding my body that it was indeed alive. Once my stomach protested at taking another bite or sip of anything, I knew I was ready to attempt to do...whatever I was going to do.

I'd never forged a connection through my tattoos like this, so I didn't have a playbook for how I would trigger this link with Logan. Finally, I settled on trying to get into the zone I found while I was tattooing—that meditative mental state that allowed me to access and apply my magic to my work.

Could I do it when I wasn't tattooing?

"One way to find out," I muttered.

I settled back into the camp chair and closed my eyes. Focusing on my breathing, I sought out that calm, assured state of mind, and surprisingly, I found it. Like when I was tattooing Logan, the connection between us stood out in my mind's eye as vividly as a glowing string of LED lights. My lips curved at the sight. The idea that the connection was there, proud and strong, filled me with satisfaction on a level

I couldn't explain. It vibrated beneath my mental fingers as I sent *I'm here* along it.

I tapped the connection again, repeating that simple phrase, and hoped it would be enough to guide Logan home.

I'm here, I'm here, I'm here.

I didn't know how much time had passed before I heard another, more significant rustle in the woods. Something larger than a squirrel or rabbit. At the same time, I realized the link had grown brighter and more intense. Opening my eyes, I lurched to my feet and caught myself on the table before I could stagger sideways. I kept my hand on the table as I made my way around it, too eager to see if Logan was coming through the woods to allow my body time to get used to moving.

"Logan?" I called.

A faint, canine grunt emanated from the woods, and my heart skipped a beat. It was him. Had to be.

"Logan!" I shouted again. "I'm here."

A wolf emerged from the trees, slowly and carefully. He was limping, not putting any weight on his right front leg, but he picked up speed as he saw me.

I stumbled down the three steps of the gazebo but managed to keep my balance enough that I didn't fall flat on my face. I sat on the second step, not trusting myself to walk on the uneven terrain toward the forest, and Logan sped up even more to meet me.

I didn't even think about it. I opened my arms to welcome him. He thrust his head against my chest, and I embraced his wonderful fluffiness, shoving my nose deep into the ruff of fur around his neck. When I'd first seen Logan and thought he'd give great hugs, this wasn't what I'd anticipated—but it *was* great, nonetheless. Then, suddenly, my arms were full of a naked man. Not that I was complaining about that development. It was a shock, that was all. With a quick repositioning, one of his arms wrapped around me in an embrace that made me feel safe and cherished. I laid my head into the crook of his neck and breathed in his essence, the scent of pine stronger than usual.

"You're awake," Logan said as he pulled back to look at me. "When did you wake up?"

"Today. Earlier. What time is it?"

"I've been a wolf for the better part of two days. I have no idea."

I chuckled. "I don't either. I'm so glad I was able to guide you here, a stór."

"I heard you. Almost like a pack bond, but not quite. Thank the goddess because I had no idea where I was."

I swept my hands over his cheeks, relishing the feel of his beard beneath my palms, then down his neck and to his shoulders. His right shoulder looked bad—discolored and swollen, though there was no sign of a bullet wound.

"I waited too long to shift," he said. "If I'd shifted immediately after, the bullet would've been forced out, but I couldn't find a spot my wolf felt was safe enough to be vulnerable like that."

"We need to take care of this."

"Yeah," he agreed with a grimace. "Someone's going to have to dig out the bullet, then I'll shift back and forth again, and the healing process will take care of the infection."

"Shit. Infection?"

"I'm running a bit hotter than usual, yeah."

With that, I noticed the heightened spots of color in his cheeks and the slight glassiness of his hazel eyes. Not good. I pulled myself to my feet and directed Logan to sit down where I'd been. It took a few seconds to transform into my human skin, then I grabbed my cell phone off the table and called Teague. He picked up on the first ring.

"I'm okay," I said to alleviate any concern. "Logan's back here, though, and he's still got the bullet in his shoulder."

"That's not good," Teague said.

"No. He's running a fever. He said someone needs to dig out the bullet so he can shift and heal properly."

"Hospital's out—"

"Hospital's definitely out," Logan butted in, reminding me he could hear the phone conversation easily.

I nodded at him to acknowledge his point. "I could try, but I don't want to fuck anything up."

"Yeah, my first aid training fell somewhat short of removing healed-over bullets." Teague paused. "Let me call Christopher and see if he has any suggestions."

"Good. Call me back." I shoved the phone into the pocket of my athletic pants and returned to Logan's side. "Let's get you cleaned up."

"There were wolves searching for me in the woods. They smelled funny." Logan lurched to his feet, much like I had a few moments before, but I was there to help steady him as we walked toward the guesthouse.

"Funny? Funny how?"

"Dunno. Funny."

I wondered if running a fever interfered with his sense of smell. Maybe. Who knew the ins and outs of werewolf physiology? "We'll get you cleaned up and into clothes, and hopefully by then, Teague will have a plan of action."

"Yeah, okay." He laid his head against mine for a

second. "I'm glad you woke up, Rian. Don't leave me alone again, 'kay?"

It was the fever talking, but the evidence that Logan had missed me still warmed my heart, even as it made the edges of it freeze. Because I was going to leave him again—either to another nap or to my full stone sleep.

Unless we figured out a loophole to this curse.

I was no stranger to blood, but seeing one of Christopher MacGrath's pack members cut into Logan's shoulder was almost more than I could take. There was nothing they could give him for the pain since his werewolf metabolism processed drugs and alcohol too quickly. So I held his good hand, enduring my own pain as his big fingers tensed and tightened. I was happy to bear it if it helped.

"Got it." The female wolf leaned back triumphantly, holding up a mangled piece of metal. I guessed she was in her forties, though it was tough to tell with werewolves. They lived longer than humans and showed signs of aging much later. She had the barest bit of gray in her glossy mahogany hair, and there were no wrinkles in her white skin. "It was in there good. I'm not sure even shifting immediately would have dislodged it."

Blood streamed down Logan's arm, thick enough that I could smell it in my human form. I was about to ask if she was going to leave him bleeding when Logan's form shimmered and morphed into his wolf. He lay on his side, the black fur covering his chest moving up and down with his labored breaths. His tongue lolled out, and his orange eyes were open a slit.

The female wolf—I hadn't caught her name—jerked

back at the change, perhaps surprised by the suddenness. She quickly recovered and turned her attention to me. "He'll need to shift back once he has the energy. That will complete the healing."

She dropped the bullet into a dish with a muffled clang, then used antiseptic wipes to get the worst of the blood off her hands before heading into the ensuite bathroom to wash up fully. We were in a bedroom at the pack's ranch, one that was amazingly unoccupied. There were about twenty wolves in the MacGrath pack—this pack, anyway. There were other MacGrath packs around the world since it was a large and well-known werewolf clan. This one was relatively small and had originally settled on the East Coast of Canada sometime in the late 1800s. Christopher, the alpha, had reached out to Teague a few years back to offer to make amends for their pack's role in our youngest brother's death centuries ago. That was how they'd ended up bound to us for the next century plus twenty-seven years. Teague was now their Príomha, a step above alpha.

The wolf exited the washroom and gave me an encouraging smile. "He'll be okay. You can stay here as long as you need to. If he doesn't shift within the next couple of hours, encourage him to. But he should do it on his own—it's instinct." She gathered up the bloodied towels she'd placed on the edge of the bed to spare the sheets, and they actually had. Her smile widened. "Look at that. Amelia won't kill me for ruining the sheets after all."

I grinned. "I'm sorry, but I missed your name."

"Not surprising. You were a little frantic when you got here." She held out a hand. "Mia."

I grasped her hand with mine. "Rian. Thank you, Mia. You saved him."

She shook her head, but I saw the faint flush on her

cheeks. "It—well, it wasn't *nothing*, but it was no worse than wounds I patched up back east. You wouldn't believe how many of these idiots got too close to farmers' herds and ended up with buckshot in their asses."

"Could you let my brothers know we'll be here a while?" As far as I knew, they were downstairs, waiting with Christopher.

"Sure thing. Like I said, as long as you need. There are clothes in the bathroom when he's ready for them, but they'll probably be a little small." She ducked out of the room and closed the door behind her with a soft click.

I let out a breath and my smile fell away. Leaning forward, I braced my head in my hands and concentrated on drawing air into my lungs and exhaling over and over again. So much had happened since I'd awoken. It was like a whirlwind. My body still ached, reminding me I'd slept for nearly five days—the longest nap yet. Did that mean my time was running out?

Wolf Logan whined. I straightened to find him watching me with those brilliant orange eyes. "I'm okay," I assured him.

He whined again as though he were calling me on my bullshit. Then he wiggled over, making more room for me in a clear invitation.

"Time for wolf cuddles?" I grinned when he huffed at me in disgust. "I love that your wolf wants to cuddle me all the time."

He grumbled, but it quickly turned into a sigh when I climbed onto the bed beside him and wove my fingers into his fur. It felt like I'd done this a few hours ago, but in reality, I knew it had been much longer than that. Days.

I wouldn't close my eyes this time. I didn't want to miss anything else.

Chapter 13

Logan

It took about an hour before I felt up to shifting back. I knew Rian was awake, watching me, which should have made returning to my naked human form awkward—but it wasn't. Following my instincts, I rolled into his arms and burrowed into his T-shirt-covered chest.

"Thank you for being here," I murmured, the words muffled by the fabric. His scent surrounded me like a comforting blanket—warm stone and the acridness of magic.

"You asked me not to leave you alone again." His words were as soothing as the hand stroking my hair. "I'm going to do my best to abide by that."

I had asked him that, hadn't I? I remembered walking out of the forest as a wolf, but everything from the moment I'd transformed into my human skin was fuzzy, from the fever, no doubt. That fog had lifted, along with the pain in my shoulder. Now that the bullet was out, I'd healed completely.

"Do you want anything to drink? Eat? Mia left some bottles of water—"

I cut him off with a kiss.

It started slow like our previous kiss, and Rian returned it without hesitation. Gentle touches of lips upon lips, tentative exploration with our tongues. But as soon as our tongues connected, the kiss exploded into something beyond gentle. Goddess, I *wanted* this man.

I rolled on top of him, bracing my arms on either side of his head as his clothes rasped against my naked skin. He opened his legs, welcoming me, and I growled into his mouth. I wasn't hard yet, but I was getting there fast, and his submission made me want to howl. Neither of us said a word as I started rocking against him, but his groan told me he was as into this turn of events as I was. Not that I'd truly doubted it, with how his mouth, lips, and tongue chased mine.

Suddenly, his skin flickered from human to living stone and back, catching me off guard. He stopped kissing abruptly, squeezing his eyes shut and pushing his head back into the pillow, panting hard. "Stop," he rasped. "We've got to—shit. Stop."

I lifted off him instantly and rolled back onto my side of the bed. "Did I hurt you?"

His eyes snapped open. "No. Gods, no." He caressed my cheek, his blunt nails scraping through my beard. "I want this. But..." He trailed off, and a pink flush rose in his cheeks. "I can't...in this form."

"You can't..." My eyes widened as the implication of his words sunk in. "You can't have sex in your human form?"

"I have to concentrate to stay in my human skin. It's not the default for us. And there's no way I can keep that focus on it when you make me feel so good."

"Damn. That complicates things, doesn't it?"

The passion leaked out of Rian's eyes, and he turned his head away from me. "I understand. It's not—"

I grabbed his chin and brought his eyes back to meet mine. "I didn't say it made me not want you anymore. It just makes it a little more complicated. Like, I'm going to have to figure out how to kiss you when you're in your living stone."

Rian's expression lightened. It wasn't quite a smile, but close. "The chin."

"The chin," I agreed, nodding. It was significant. "We'll figure it out."

"Yeah?" That was hope in his eyes, which made me wonder...

"Have you been intimate with anyone since the curse?"

"No. I tried once. We'd been run out of a village after Drew attempted to have sex with someone and discovered he couldn't hold on to his human form. But I thought, hey, that's Drew. Maybe it would be different for me." He twisted up his lips. "Spoiler alert: it wasn't. But I stopped the encounter when I felt my control slipping, and she never knew the difference."

"She?"

He traced a finger over my wrinkled brow. "I'm pansexual. Of course, I didn't have a word for it until this time awake. But I've always liked people—it never mattered their shape, size, or gender. Is that a problem?"

"Of course not."

The blush, which had faded, came roaring back. "Uh. So I should probably tell you I've never...with a man."

"Never...?" I prompted.

"Gone all the way?" He rolled his eyes. "That sounds so bad. I've kissed one or two, lusted after far more, but nothing beyond that."

Why did that make my wolf rumble in pleasure? I

wasn't so animalistic that I felt satisfied to be his first venture into male-on-male sex, was I? Clearly, I was, because the thought of it revived my cock.

"Your eyes changed to orange for a second." Rian smirked. "You liked that revelation, didn't you?"

"No comment." I rolled away from him to hide my returned erection. "We shouldn't do any more here, anyway. Not when we're surrounded by werewolves who can hear everything. And smell it too."

He wrinkled his nose. "Ew."

"But when we get back to your guesthouse, let's explore this, okay?" I paused. "If you're up for it, I mean. How are you feeling?"

"Fine enough to take you up on that offer." He waggled his brows. "Go have a shower. Mia said earlier that there are sweats and a T-shirt on the counter in the bathroom, though she warned they might not fit."

"Anything's better than walking around naked, covered in blood." I frowned at the itchiness of the dried blood on my arm. "I'll be quick."

"Take your time."

I didn't intend on luxuriating under the shower, but once the warm water started pouring down on me, I couldn't help it. After two nights in the woods, battling pain and a fever, the cascade of water—at the perfect pressure, I might add—was incredible.

The clothes left for me were not.

They weren't new, going by how the fabric was pilled in places, but the sweatpants were tight enough that they rode up the crack of my ass and the T-shirt threatened to strangle me. But I could forgive them anything when I emerged from the bathroom and Rian's eyes warmed with appreciation.

"Very nice."

I focused on helping myself to a bottle of water so he wouldn't see how my cheeks had reddened with the compliment. Usually, comments about my body made me uncomfortable. It was always the only thing people saw—my height, my weight, my "bear" status. Rian's praise felt different, maybe because I knew he saw *me* first and appreciated my body second.

Ugh. Psychoanalysis was so not my field.

After drinking a second bottle of water and pulling at the T-shirt's neck and chest to stretch it a bit, I felt ready to leave the unfamiliar bedroom and retreat to the guesthouse, a sanctuary I missed. Odd—I'd been away from it for two nights, but it felt far longer. I didn't miss my condo nearly as much.

Mia spotted us as we made our way down the stairs. "You're looking good," she said, and I knew she wasn't talking about the clothes. "Good color, steady. How do you feel?"

"Good as new. Thank you so much."

She dismissed my words with a wave of her hand. "Any time. I mean, don't make it a habit, but I'm here to help whenever you need it."

"I appreciate that." Her offer sparked a spot of warmth in my chest, knowing this was what a true pack was—a collective of people helping each other. I'd never had that. Family, sure. I'd considered Mom and Lyle my pack, but it wasn't quite the same.

"Príomha and Alpha are in the lounge, along with your other brother," she told Rian, pointing to the right.

He shot her a smile. "Thanks."

She headed off in the opposite direction with a wave.

I subtly sniffed the air as we reached the bottom of the

stairs. Although Mia was no longer in sight, her scent remained. And it wasn't right.

I remembered I'd hidden in the woods rather than let the strange wolves find me. I hadn't seen them, but I'd smelled them, and there was something so unnatural about their scents that my wolf had decided to avoid them at all costs. It wasn't the fever messing with my senses because Mia smelled the same now. It was hard to describe in human terms but like a twisted version of a wolf. As though her scent had once been *other* but manipulated into something close to—but not quite—a canine's. Other shifters might not notice, but as a wolf, I certainly did.

None of the brothers knew. They'd all referred to the pack as werewolves and made no mention of this oddity. My skin crawled at the idea that this entire pack was deceiving the gargoyles—unless there was another explanation, my rational mind interjected. Maybe there was, and I wasn't seeing it.

I hoped that was the case. But there was no way I could leave the wolves' ranch without making sure the brothers knew their allies may not be who they seemed.

Rian led me to the lounge, which matched the décor of the rest of the house—rustic, with polished wood, leather seating, and the occasional rugged fabric, like the chair with woven upholstery. The room was large enough to house two couches and two chairs on either end, making an inviting conversation area. A scuffed and worn area rug covered the wood floor beneath the seating, showing me that this room was well-used and not solely for guests. A lit fireplace on the far end of the room sent warmth cascading through it, making the space even more welcoming.

Teague sat on one of the couches in his police uniform, rumpled from a day's wear, while Drew and Josh sat on the other couch, their heads together as they spoke quietly. Three cups of coffee in various states of emptiness were on the table separating the couches, adding a rich undertone to the leather-and-wood scent of the room. A man I hadn't met, with a similar scent to Mia's, occupied one of the chairs on the side of the couches farthest from the entryway. He wore a green-and-blue flannel shirt and medium-wash jeans. Though he was sitting, I could tell he was of significant height, with a muscular build—the way his clothes stretched across his chest and the pale, worn spots on the thighs of his jeans said as much. He was white, with messy brown hair and a beard that cascaded down his neck to meet with chest hair jutting from the collar of the navy-blue T-shirt he wore beneath his flannel. What made me pause was his brilliant, clear amber eyes—the sign of an alpha wolf.

Was I wrong in my theory?

Rian's brothers grinned at our entry and rose to greet us, doling out hugs and backslaps. I couldn't help but smile when Josh stood on his tip-toes to grab my face with both hands and inspect it.

"You ruined your haircut." He wrinkled his nose. "Probably your mani-pedi too."

I swept a hand through my damp hair to tousle it, and Josh released my face. "I didn't have my styling products with me. It's not ruined."

"But you're not arguing about the mani-pedi."

I wrinkled my nose. "Yeah, no, that's probably done for. Walking through the woods in bare feet will do that."

"All of Haider's hard work..."

"We'll have to go back."

He brightened. "Yeah? You'd want to do that?"

"I would."

"Well then."

"Maybe we could bring Rian and Drew. Make it a double date."

Drew immediately raised his hands in a stop gesture. "Hell no."

Josh latched onto his arm. "Oh, come on. It'd be fun."

Rian shrugged. "I'm down."

"Do you see these hands?" Drew held one up in front of his partner's face. The nails had chips here and there and dark spots on the skin that smelled of oil. "These are not hands that need a manicure. They're working hands."

"Working hands need the most care," Josh countered.

Teague cleared his throat. "As fascinating as this conversation is," he said, with a brow raised in case any of us missed his sarcasm, "I believe introductions are in order."

I stepped around the table to join Teague where he stood with Christopher MacGrath. The alpha smiled at me, his demeanor open and welcoming. I wouldn't know he was lying about anything without being able to scent him. At that thought, anger swelled in my chest, bringing with it the need to protect my almost-pack.

"Christopher MacGrath, alpha of the MacGrath pack," Teague said, gesturing between MacGrath and me. "Professor Logan Davis."

MacGrath held out a hand, his smile dimming slightly as he caught the scent of my anger. "A pleasure, Professor."

I gripped his hand but didn't shake. "I wish I could say the same. What are you?"

"I don't know—"

"Don't bullshit me. The nose knows." He tried to pull away, but I tightened my hand on his. "What are you, MacGrath? Because you're not a werewolf."

Chapter 14

Rian

Christopher wasn't a werewolf? That made no sense. He was a member of the MacGrath pack, who we had a long history with. Of course, he was a werewolf.

Except there was something in his eyes that told me Logan's accusation had struck a nerve. Fear, maybe? It was quickly replaced by defiance and anger as he yanked his hand out of Logan's tight grip.

"My pack patches you up, and *this* is how you repay us? With baseless accusations?" Christopher snarled. "You're ridiculous."

Teague, ever the peacekeeper, stepped up to the two men—not between them because he wasn't that reckless. "Christopher, I understand you're upset, but I don't believe Logan would say this without basis. Logan?"

"You're going to listen to him before you listen to me?" Christopher's amber eyes narrowed—but despite his heightened emotions, they weren't glowing. Odd.

"I want to know why Logan said what he did, to allow you a chance to provide a rebuttal."

"They smell wrong," Logan stated, his gaze never leaving Christopher. "On the surface, like wolves, but underneath, it's twisted and...wrong." He glanced at Teague. "Sorry, it's not easy to describe in human terms. But it's definitely not normal."

"Could it be the difference between this pack and others you're used to?"

Logan shook his head before Teague finished the sentence. "No. I've met many other werewolves, and none smelled like this."

"And you're going to trust his word? You've known him for what, a week?" Christopher scoffed.

"I trust him," I stated.

Drew glared at Christopher. Of the three of us, he'd been the slowest to accept the MacGrath pack into our lives. "And why would he lie? What does he have to gain?"

"Our land—"

Logan snorted. "I don't want your property. I have no intention of living here."

Oh. That hurt. But now wasn't the time to dwell on that statement, so I shoved the pain aside.

"I don't want to take over your pack—I'm not even an alpha," Logan continued. "All I want is to protect Rian, Teague, Drew, and Josh. They've been nothing but kind to me, and they deserve to find happiness."

"There's an easy way to solve this," Drew said. "Shift."

"I've shifted in your presence before—"

"Yeah, when we were getting *shot at*," Drew countered. "None of us were paying attention to you."

It had been at the ceremony that bound Christopher and his pack to us for the next one hundred and twenty-seven years. The pride had interjected themselves at the very end, thankfully after the bonding had taken.

"I'm not a trick pony," Christopher insisted.

Despite the anger in his tone, his eyes still weren't glowing. I glanced at Teague to see if he'd noticed, and his scowl said he had. Of course—close observation was what he did for a living.

"As your Príomha, I'm asking you to shift for us." Teague's voice was low and gravely serious.

"Príomha?" Logan asked me with a frown.

"Teague's the alpha of alphas, so that's what they call him. Technically, the four of us"—I waved at my brothers and Josh—"are alphas above the pack."

Logan's frown deepened. "That's not possible."

"There was a ceremony with their Moon Speaker and—"

"Their what?"

For the first time, real unease wriggled in my gut. "Their Moon Speaker. They were like a shaman. Dressed in furs and—Logan!"

He'd spun, grabbed Christopher by the neck, and shoved him against a portion of the wall that held no bookcases. A painting next to them swung back and forth before clattering to the floor. "Who the *fuck* are you? Answer me!"

I raced forward and seized Logan's arm. "What are you—"

"There are no shamans in wolf packs. No one can wield magic. Our magic is our ability to shift and heal, and that's it. We have healers, like Mia, but their skills are mundane." He shook Christopher. "What did you do to the brothers?"

The ruckus had attracted other pack members at the door. Two of his enforcers, Milo and Gage, started to push through the crowd. With a glance, Drew manipulated any metal they wore into bindings, holding them in place.

"Well done." I was impressed and not afraid to let my

brother know it. Before breaking the curse, he'd had to touch metal to change its shape. Now, it appeared his ability had grown.

"Thanks. Been practicing."

Christopher jerked his gaze from his immobilized enforcers—who now conveniently blocked the entry of anyone else—back to Logan and Teague. "Didn't hurt you," he managed to squeeze out past Logan's hand on his throat. "Never our intent."

"What did you do?" Logan defined each word with a growl. Unlike Christopher's unlit amber eyes, Logan's were blazing orange.

"What I needed to do to help my family."

Not *pack*. Family. That one simple word told me all I needed to know.

Logan was right.

Holy. Shit.

"Teague?" I couldn't keep the worry from my voice. We'd fallen for Christopher's story, hook, line, and sinker. What did that mean for *my* family?

"Logan, put him down."

With a second's hesitation, Logan followed Teague's order and released his grip on Christopher's neck. A red mark in the shape of Logan's hand circled the pale skin of Christopher's throat—a mark that showed no sign of vanishing. It should have started fading as soon as Logan let go, thanks to werewolf healing.

"Shift," Teague ordered Christopher.

Drew stepped forward. "Do it, or I'll pull out every ounce of iron from your body."

My eyes widened. Damn, could he do that? If nothing else, it was an excellent threat.

Christopher thought so too because he began stripping

out of his clothes. None of us turned our eyes away, unwilling to have him out of our direct sight for any length of time.

I'd seen Logan transform into his wolf more than once now. The transition was seamless—one moment, he was human, and the next, he was wolf. There was nothing about it that looked painful or strenuous. It was natural and yet, magical.

Christopher's shift was nothing like it.

Whereas Logan's shift was nearly instantaneous, Christopher's appeared much slower. If I hadn't had Logan's shift to compare it to, I wouldn't necessarily understand how labored Christopher's was. There was no natural flow from one form to the next. It looked like a struggle, as though he were fighting his nature. Finally, his shift was done, and the difference Logan had caught in the wolf's scent became clear.

Christopher's wolf was much smaller than Logan's, slightly more than half his size. His shape was...not *wrong*, but subtly not right either. His legs were shorter, his snout blunter, his tail almost cropped. He looked like someone who'd seen a wolf once and had tried putting one together from memory. It was close enough to what a wolf should look like that someone who didn't have time to examine him or saw him in passing might accept his appearance.

In other words, it was meant to fool us.

"Holy shit, Logan was right," Josh whispered.

Teague had gone stone-faced. Any other time, I might giggle internally at the pun, but not today. Given my brother's ability to feel others' emotions, he'd learned to lock down his own. When he locked them down this hard, I knew he was feeling strongly. Deeply.

Right now, I imagined it was betrayal. It sliced through

me as well. But it had been Teague who'd brought the MacGrath pack—or whoever these people were—into our lives. He'd thought it was a chance to forge an allyship with a group motivated to abide by the agreement.

But if the ritual to bind the pack to us had been a sham, what had it actually done? Because it had done *something*. I'd seen the magic race from the Moon Speaker, or whoever the fuck they were, through Teague and into Christopher.

Drew let loose with a string of Irish curses I hadn't heard in years. If Teague was stone-faced, Drew was absolutely molten with rage. He stepped forward, menace in every line of his body, halting when Josh strengthened his hold on his arm.

"We trusted you, you son of a bitch," he spat. "We believed you when you said you wanted to make up for your pack's history. And it's all a lie?"

Christopher's shift back to human was as painful-looking as the previous one. I half expected him to have something wrong with his human visage as there'd been with his wolf, but he looked the same as ever—white skin, scruffy brown hair and beard, and—wait.

His eyes were no longer amber. Teague stepped forward and retrieved something from the floor—a contact lens with amber coloring.

"I can explain," Christopher said, a slight tremor in his voice as he pulled his underwear back on.

"I highly fuckin' doubt that," Drew snarled.

"Drew..." Josh stroked his partner's upper arm, but it did little to console my hot-tempered brother.

"No, Josh. They did some magic to us—to you! If it wasn't what they told us it was, then what was it? Are we in danger?"

By *we*, he meant Josh. His blue eyes held worry and

love in equal measure. I had never thought Drew would fall so hard for someone, but I was so glad he had.

There was a commotion at the door, and I turned to find Mia had shoved her way between Milo and Gage's immobile forms and gotten stuck there. "There's no danger to any of you."

"Mia—" Christopher growled.

"No, you bullheaded idiot. I told you this was going to bite you in the ass."

"Or throat," Logan rumbled, his eyes a steady orange.

Man, I really shouldn't have found his willingness to defend us so hot.

Christopher finished pulling his pants on and slowly sank to the floor, cupping his forehead in his palms. "Fuck," he muttered. "Fuck, fuck, fuck."

"He needs fluids. Something to eat," Mia stated. "I can bring him some."

For the first time, Teague shot her a look. He'd lost his human skin at some point and his eyes were blazing violet. When he spoke, it was nearly as deep a rumble as Logan's. "No." He turned back to Christopher. "I demand an explanation. *Now!*"

A force burst out of my brother, rattling the bookshelves around the room and the abandoned coffee mugs on the table between the couches. I'd felt this once before. When we'd awoken to find our brother, Odhrán, was nothing more than dust. Teague's reaction had surprised us all. Pure rage. For an instant, as it passed through me, it ratcheted my own anger to an unspeakable level. Then it was gone, and I heaved out a breath.

Christopher looked up at Teague with fear in his unremarkable brown eyes. "You're right. We're not wolves. And we're not MacGrath." He inhaled, the air shuddering in his chest. "My name is Christian Holt. This is my sleuth—not my pack."

They were bears? What the...?

"But each person in this house is a member of my family, which is more important than being part of a sleuth. Mia is my older sister. Everyone else is cousins, uncles, aunts. All related."

"*Why?*" The word jolted from my lips. It was the one question we needed an answer to beyond all else.

"Gods." He leaned his head against the wall, looking up at the ceiling. "It's not a simple answer."

Teague's eyes flared impossibly brighter. "Tell us."

"About thirty years ago, my asshole of a father slept with the wrong girl. And she was a girl—only nineteen. She fell pregnant and came to him, hoping for a happily ever after. Instead, he told her he didn't want another fuckin' mouth to feed, she wasn't anything to him but a one-and-done, and if she didn't want the kid, she should get an abortion.

"Being nineteen and still living with her parents, I assume she felt that getting an abortion would be too diffi-cult and having a baby would be too embarrassing, so she killed herself."

"Oh my god," Josh whispered. "Trigger warning, man."

"You wanted to know."

Drew glared at Christo—Christian. "Go on, asshole."

"Her father wanted revenge. She was above the age of consent and an adult, so despite the age difference—my dad was in his fifties at the time—there was no legal recourse. But, as it turned out, the family came from a long line of kitchen witches. Her father exploited that background, building it however he could until he had enough knowl-edge and power to curse my dad and everyone who bore his blood."

"Fuckin' curses," Drew muttered.

"What was the curse?" Teague demanded.

"It stole our bears. It couldn't erase our nature as shifters, but it diminished it, warped it. As a result, there hasn't been a child born in our family since the curse took hold."

"And your father?" Josh asked.

"Dead. The girl's father used Dad's blood, as well as his own, to power the curse." For the first time since he'd started the story, Christian met Teague's fiery gaze. "It wasn't enough for him to kill Dad. The bastard wanted to ensure his family was tortured before we all die too."

Teague crossed his arms. "And where does your deception come in?"

Christian sighed. "I've been looking for a way to reverse the spell since I was old enough to lead the family—so, for about twenty years. Fifteen years ago, a seer shared a prophecy with me." He cleared his throat. "'Brothers three, cast in stone; follow them, and they'll lead you home.'"

"Oh, it rhymes and everything," Drew said with heavy sarcasm. "It must be true."

"They shared other visions with me that made me trust them," Christian countered. "Including a vision of a gargoyle with purple eyes. That's what eventually led me to you. I thought you would be close to us in New Brunswick, but none of the other shifter clans had ever heard of a trio of gargoyles. Until I asked the MacGrath pack." His lips pressed into a thin line. "They knew the legend of the gargoyles they betrayed, and be thankful it wasn't actually Christopher MacGrath who reached out to you. He is a grade-A prick who told me the story of what they'd done to you—told me proudly, I might add, and preened when I said I was going to include it in a book of legends for the paranormal community. Much like his predecessors, he isn't the sharpest tool in the shed."

"And with that story in hand, you had your opening." Teague's shoulders deflated, and I imagined it was because he blamed himself for falling for Christian's ruse. But how could he not? He hadn't wanted to involve us in the early discussions with who he thought was Christopher MacGrath, knowing Drew and I would be less than receptive to the idea of the pack as allies, given our history with them. They'd been responsible for Odhrán's death. But Teague hadn't been wrong—we *did* need allies as we moved along into the future. The pride's presence illustrated that.

"I did. I felt that if I reached out to you with the truth, you'd turn us away, and you're our one chance at removing this curse before it wipes out my family line."

"Because he's an idiot," Mia shouted from the doorway.

Christian stood, using the wall to balance himself. He probably really did need fluids and energy, given how difficult his shifts looked. "Maybe I am. But I couldn't take the chance. I would do anything to save my family, Teague. I *will* do anything."

"Including infecting us with unknown magic," Drew snarled.

"Not all of you." Christian leaned back against the wall. "The spell bound Teague and me, that's all."

In an instant, I saw red. "That's all? That's *all?*" I lurched toward him, only stopping because Logan forcefully held me back. "What did you do to him?"

"I joined our souls." Christian lifted his chin defiantly. "If I die, he dies."

Chapter 15

Logan

Since I was the one to instigate that shitshow, it seemed fair that I was the one to herd the brothers and Josh out of the ranch before someone could do something they regretted. None of them were thinking clearly, though I couldn't blame them. Even Josh, who had always struck me as level-headed, was so furious he was shaking. Drew held his hand in a white-knuckled grip while Rian draped an arm over Teague's shoulders. He whispered something in Teague's ear, but I purposefully didn't listen to what he was saying.

The brothers had had their trust broken enough for one day.

Once we arrived at the mansion, I followed them inside instead of aiming for the guesthouse. I had a feeling I might be needed as a mediator or a calming influence. Not that I wasn't angry on their behalf—especially Rian's—but I had more distance from my emotions, even if I was feeling more than I had in months.

Drew stormed into the kitchen, rage in every line of his body. He kicked one of the stools at the island. They were heavy metal stools, no doubt designed to take a gargoyle's weight, and it landed on the tile floor with an ominous *crunch.*

"God fucking *dammit!*" He wasn't cursing about the broken tile—I doubt he realized he'd broken it. "I told you. *I told you* we couldn't trust them!"

"When you thought they were MacGrath wolves," Teague countered. In contrast to Drew, it seemed as though the rage and fight had drained out of Teague entirely.

"Obviously, it's shifters in general we can't trust."

"Hey," Rian snapped. "Don't be a generalizing ass."

Some of the fire left Drew's expression. "Sorry, Logan."

I nodded. "Apology accepted. I swear we're not all bad. We're just people. I think you attract the ones with ulterior motives because of who you are and maybe what you represent."

"And what do we represent?" Rian asked.

"Magic. A magic beyond anything a shifter will—or should—ever know. You're not human, but not shifters, and yet, you can shift, and *yet*, you can do magic." I shrugged. "I'm not saying it's logical or even a conscious recognition, but there's even a part of me that's awed to be in your presence."

"Regardless of why, we've now got another group of shifters acting against us." Rian grabbed one of his horns.

"I don't think so." I drew in a breath. "Look, can we go sit in the living room? Talk about this as rationally and objectively as possible?"

Drew snorted as he helped Josh right the stool, and Josh elbowed him. "Behave." He groaned at the floor. "Ah, damn, Drew. The tile shattered."

"Sorry."

"If you wanted new tiles in the kitchen, all you had to do was ask."

Drew wrapped Josh in a giant hug. "I'm sorry."

I left them to his apologies and followed the others into the living room. It looked like a typical living room in a typical Canadian home. The couch and chairs were all overstuffed and perhaps oversized for the space, but when you had three gargoyle brothers using them, they needed to be sturdy. I, for one, appreciated the brothers' tendency to go for large pieces of furniture. Too often, I found trendy furniture questionable, with its delicate stature and size.

Teague collapsed into one of the chairs and leaned his head back. I took one side of the couch, pleasantly surprised when Rian sat beside me, his thigh pressed against mine. He was crowding my space, but he'd get no complaint from me. Josh and Drew joined us a few minutes later with glasses of ice water on a tray.

"Nothing stronger?" Teague asked.

Josh shot him a look. "Discussing this rationally, as Logan requested, won't happen if we douse ourselves in alcohol."

"Maybe I'm tired of being rational and logical."

"Aren't we all," Rian interjected sardonically.

Josh took the other end of the couch and Drew the remaining chair. For a second, I wondered at that—then I noticed the pinkness of Josh's lips and the fresh beard burn on his neck and cheeks. A quick scent of the air confirmed it, and I reached for one of the glasses to hide my twitching lips. Drew and Josh had taken a few moments for themselves in the kitchen and no doubt needed to cool off.

I sipped the water, gathering my thoughts and turning them back to the crisis at hand. "I don't think you have to worry about fighting the Holt family."

Any softness in Drew's expression fled. "They betrayed us."

"There's no arguing that. They absolutely did," Rian said. "But I get what Logan's saying. They could have acted against us at any point in the past two months, and they haven't."

"They could be biding their time."

"More likely, they're trying to follow you, like the seer told Christian," I said.

"So fucking stupid," Drew growled. "How could they believe that nonsense?"

"Because they're desperate," Josh said. "Desperate people do desperate things. You heard Christo—Christian. He'd do anything to save his family."

Drew frowned at his partner. "You sound like you're...*sympathetic* to him."

Josh glared right back. "Get that stupid thought out of your head, mister. Yes, I'm sympathetic. I'm not whatever other word you wanted to say there. I don't agree with what he did, and I'm always, *always* on the side of my family."

Drew let out a breath. "Sorry."

"You're going to wear that word out today, dearthàir." Rian smirked.

"Trasna ort féin, *dearthàir*," Drew shot back.

"So." I raised my voice to cut off any further banter between Drew and Rian, as amusing as it was. "I say we focus on solving our most pressing problem."

"The Fomori and the pride," Rian said.

"Exactly. Christian may still help us with that."

Drew scoffed. "As if I'd trust those assholes to have our backs."

"Your feelings aren't invalid, but remember—they're motivated to follow you. They're looking for the salvation of their family, and they believe following you will lead them there. I think you can trust that their motivation will remain strong and aligned with your goals."

"Maybe." Drew sank back against the chair with a grumble.

"Have you made any progress on your research?" Josh asked.

It felt like it had been months since I'd even looked at the copious notes and books strewn across the guesthouse table. I cast my brain back to the latest nuggets of information we'd uncovered and suddenly remembered what I'd gleaned from our confrontation with Becker along the highway. "Oh shit, my theory."

"Your what?" Rian asked.

"Josh told me about witnessing the Fomori force a shift on one of the bikers. Have you ever witnessed any of the cats shift other than that?"

Each brother's brow furrowed as they presumably thought back over their encounters.

"We didn't see it," Rian finally said, "but after the pride shot up our bonding ceremony with the wolves, we heard a mountain lion scream. I assume they shifted once confronted by Christo—Christian's wol—fuck. Whatever they are."

"Interesting." I took a moment to turn that info around in my head. "When Becker confronted us on the highway, I taunted him to shift and fight me."

Rian jerked away so he could face me. "I'm sorry. You did *what*?"

"That's why I was shifted. I was about ninety percent certain he wouldn't shift, but even if he had, I felt I had pretty good odds against him."

"Pretty good?" Rian echoed.

I patted his hand somewhat awkwardly.

"Your theory?" Teague prompted.

"The Fomori controls their shifts. I think Becker entered into an agreement with her, where she would help them take over Arrington, and didn't read the fine print."

"That's why you mentioned loopholes to Becker and his sidekick." Josh shot me a sheepish grin when I raised my brows. "I might have had the window rolled down so I could hear."

"Right, exactly. Loopholes. I don't think Becker was specific enough in his agreement, so the Fomori is essentially controlling the pride."

"Can we use that?" Rian asked.

"I'm not sure. It might depend on how she's controlling them. For example, does she need to be present to allow them to shift? Or can she give advance permission?"

"Remember when the pride shot up our ritual with the pack?" Josh shook his head. "I know they're not a pack, but whatever. The mountain lion shifted when the wolves caught up to them. We all heard the cat's scream. The Fomori could have been there, or nearby. We didn't know about her involvement until about a week later."

"The"—I paused, raising my hands to make air quotes—"'wolves' didn't report scenting anything unusual?"

"No," Drew said. "But looking back, they'd found their target, so they might not have noticed anything else."

"And who knows if their senses are what they should be, with their shifted form so messed up," Rian added.

"Good point," I said. "Still probably better than a human's or yours."

"Teague?" Rian watched his oldest brother with concern clear in his red-tinged eyes. I understood why—more than any of the brothers, Teague had believed Christian's story, and he was the one whose soul was now bound to the pseudo-wolf's. "What do you think?"

Teague let out a long, slow breath. "I think I'm going to go to bed."

Neither Drew nor Rian protested, despite it being 4 p.m. They silently watched Teague heft himself out of his chair and trudge off toward the stairs.

"I've never seen him like this," Rian said quietly once we heard Teague reach the second floor.

"Not even after Odhrán," Drew agreed. "I could kill MacGrath. Holt. Whatever the fuck his name is."

Josh gave his partner a recriminating look. "Kill's a bit strong, don't you think?"

Drew grunted. "Maim, then."

Rian leaned back into the couch, his shoulder brushing mine. "Definitely maim."

"I'd be down for that option." I raised my brows again as Drew, Josh, and Rian all looked at me in surprise. "What?"

"You're like the least bloodthirsty wolf I've ever met," Rian said.

"I know. But..." I trailed off, trying to put my thoughts in order so I could explain myself in human terms. "You magically adopted me, right?"

"Unintentionally, but yes." He clarified for the others, "I tattooed Logan, and it connected us. Somehow."

"Lots of nonconsensual magical bonding going around," Drew grumbled.

Rian grimaced. "Yeah."

"It's fine. Truly. It was...it is exactly what I need." I took in a steadying breath. "I lost my mom and twin brother within the past six months. Mom had fast-acting cancer, and Lyle was in a car accident."

"I'm so sorry," Josh said.

"Thank you. It's been hard because they weren't just my family but my pack. I didn't even realize how much I needed that connection until Rian forged one with me. And through him, to all of you. You're my almost-pack."

Rian smiled. "Almost-pack. I like that."

"So do I." Drew shocked me with his approval. Given his animosity toward Christian's "wolves," I thought he'd be more resistant to my claim. Maybe he read something of my surprise on my face because he continued, "You're a good guy, Logan. You bring a needed balance to this family."

My eyes widened. "Oh, I—"

Rian gripped and squeezed my hand, cutting off my words. "I agree."

Oh no. I'd given the wrong impression. "I meant, it'll help when I go back to Victoria."

Those words were like a bomb in the room. Drew locked eyes with Rian—I'm not sure what silent communication they shared, but after a moment, Drew stood and held out a hand to Josh. "Help me make dinner?"

Josh's gaze darted between Drew and Rian, and finally, he sighed, muttering something about stoic alpha males under his breath. "We should talk more tomorrow. Do some real planning," he said as he rose.

"Sure. We'll come over after breakfast," Rian said before looking at me. "You ready to go home?"

Home. The guesthouse. I should have resisted the nomenclature and corrected him, but I didn't. The guesthouse did feel like home, as much as I wanted to protest otherwise. I had a feeling Rian had used that term on purpose too.

I wouldn't argue it. For now.

———

MUCH LIKE I imagined Drew and Josh were doing, Rian and I worked together to make dinner. It was a simple meal —pork chops with a creamy mushroom sauce, rice, and broiled brussels sprouts—and we didn't discuss any heavy topics while preparing it or eating. It was so nice to be in his presence after nearly five days without him that I didn't want any of the recent chaos to intrude on this shared moment. The urgency I'd felt to *go all the way* with him—I grinned as I remembered the flush in Rian's cheeks as he used that phrase—had dimmed but not disappeared completely. For the moment, though, I was content to talk with him, be near him, and indulge in casual touches I hadn't had with anyone for so long.

Like holding his hand as we walked around the brothers' property after we ate. Such a simple thing, and yet, it felt profound to my wolf and me. I wasn't lying when I shared that I hadn't realized how desperately I needed a connection to another living being. On some level, I'd known my wolf was hurting, but my brain was so foggy with grief that I didn't recognize why. Now the fog was lifting, and for the first time in half a year, I could almost see my way back to myself. Not the same self I'd been before losing Mom and Lyle, but a version closer than the overwhelmed and subdued person I'd been for months.

A significant contributor to that change was the horned man holding my hand.

Impulsively, I raised our hands and kissed his gray knuckles.

Rian smiled, the expression transforming his horrific visage as it always did. "What was that for?"

"To thank you."

He ducked his head. "Not sure you should thank me for anything. I've definitely made your life more troublesome."

"Maybe. But also more interesting."

"That's one way to put it." He kicked at a cluster of pine cones on the path.

"You gave me space to find myself too."

"Yeah, well…"

"And support."

He stopped and faced me. "Are you breaking up with me?"

"What? No."

"Because it sounds like you're building up to an 'it's not you, it's me' defense."

Still holding Rian's hand, I pushed him off the trail and pressed his back against a convenient lodgepole pine. The tree shook with the impact, and a pine cone landed with a subdued thud beside us. I lifted his hands above his horns and held them against the rough bark.

"Does this feel like I'm breaking up with you?" I nosed at his cheek, my breath whispering past his ear.

"N-no," he admitted shakily.

I fought my instincts to ravage and claim, pulling back so I could see his face. "Is this okay?"

His pupils were blown wide as he gazed up at me. He'd abandoned his human form long ago, safe as we were on the brothers' property. "Fuck yes, this is okay."

"Good."

I dipped down and captured his mouth. Or, well, I tried to. It wasn't easy to figure out a way to kiss him, but I managed by tilting my head to make room for his chin. There was no need to muffle ourselves or hold back if we didn't want to. No one was around to hear or scent us—my senses told me so. My tongue speared into his mouth, unrelenting. He met me thrust for thrust, his desire as fervent as my own until we were panting from exertion.

I fell to my knees, ignoring the roughness of the forest floor digging through my jeans, and tugged his athletic pants down around his thighs. He wore no underwear beneath them. Saliva flooded my mouth as I got my first glimpse at Rian's cock—uncut and strangely gray, though much darker than the rest of his skin, and the perfect medium between thin and thick, short and long. Instead of all but scorching my hand, as a human cock would, it was lukewarm at best. Rather than velvet over steel, his living stone skin was rougher and felt thicker under my palm.

I couldn't wait to get him in my mouth.

"That's about as hard as I'll—*Críost*, Logan!" Rian shouted as I took him as deep as I could.

Blowing a dick made out of stone was going to take some practice. It didn't have as much give as a human penis. Scraping my teeth against his length wasn't going to hurt him, but it might hurt *me*. I focused on sucking and using my tongue, rationalizing that he'd need more pressure and force to truly feel what I was doing.

I was right.

"Fuck, Logan. Fuck. Don't stop." Rian's litany of pleas continued, growing more nonsensical until they devolved into whines and whimpers as the sensations overwhelmed him.

The idea that I was doing this to him, that I was the one ripping those sounds from his chest...it was hot as hell. I scrambled to undo my jeans and pull my hard-as-a-rock dick out, knowing that if I didn't, I would likely make a mess in my underwear. The slight bite to the evening air couldn't dim my arousal, especially not when Rian's taloned fingers slid through my hair and held on for dear life.

If my mouth wasn't full, I'd probably be as vocal as he was. My wolf rumbled in approval, which added vibrations to my repertoire of blowjob skills, an addition Rian seemed to greatly appreciate, given how his grip on my hair tightened.

"Gonna," he panted.

My wolf growled. *Want.* I sucked hard, needing to taste Rian as much as my wolf did.

Rian tensed a second before his essence exploded across my tongue. I swallowed every spurt eagerly, enjoying the bitter, salty taste edged with a hint of stone and ozone. The end result of blowjobs was never my favorite part—usually, I pulled off and let my partner shoot into the air. But I was hungry for Rian's release. Desperate for it.

My cock spasmed in my hand, and I came with a gasp. I grunted around Rian's dick as my own emptied, pleasure ricocheting through me. Everything around me dimmed into unimportance, except for the erection I held lovingly between my lips. I returned to myself slowly, realizing I was licking Rian's length clean as he shuddered beneath my touch.

"Too much?" My voice was harsh, thanks to the roughness in my throat.

Rian's head was tilted back against the tree, his eyes closed. "No. Feels good. So fuckin' good."

I smiled and continued, happy I'd satisfied my ma—

Oh *no.*

Chapter 16

Rian

Someone knocking on the door at 3 a.m. was never good.

"Wha's that?" Logan slurred next to me. He'd fallen asleep hours ago after I'd returned the pleasure of the blowjob he'd given me in the woods. Which I hadn't intended to be the locale where we shared our first time together, but hey, I wasn't complaining.

I, on the other hand, hadn't slept at all. After a five-day "nap," I didn't need any more rest. "I'll check it out. Go back to sleep." I nuzzled his cheek—the best I could do with the stupid shape of my gargoyle face—and he rumbled in approval before drifting off again.

I pulled on the pants I'd hastily discarded on the floor and a zip-up hoodie, which I left open. The only people who'd rap on the door at this time of night were my brothers or Josh, and they were all used to the overly casual states of dress while we were at home.

The knocking started again as I reached the door, and I pulled it open abruptly so it wouldn't wake Logan again.

Josh stood in the doorway, wearing sweatpants and a fleece sweater. My heart skipped a beat at the serious look on his face. "Everything okay?"

"Drew and Teague are fine," he rushed to assure me. "But we've got a situation."

"What sort of situation?"

"Pride defectors?" He gave me an unsure smile. "You should come meet with them. Logan too."

"Are we sure this isn't some sort of a...a ruse?"

"I don't know. They seem genuine." He frowned, likely remembering that the "pack" had seemed genuine as well. "Logan will probably be able to sniff out if they aren't."

"Good point." As much as I hated to wake him, we needed both his analytical mind and sharp senses. "Give us five."

"Yeah, okay. I'll let Drew know." Josh turned to leave, then spun around with a smirk. "By the way, how hard did Logan have to bite to leave that mark on your pec?"

I jerked my head down to look at my chest, and sure enough, there was a darker indentation right above my heart. "Fuck you," I said without heat.

He laughed as he started for the main house.

THE MOUNTAIN LION shifters sitting around the backyard patio were quite the ragtag group. Teague and Drew were off to the side, watching them as they waited for Josh, Logan, and me but keeping their distance. There was an older Black guy with tight gray curls who could be anywhere from fifty to seventy. A white teenager with zits on his cheeks sat next to him, leaning against his side. There were two women, one with white skin and the other with brown, who looked to be about in their thirties, sitting with their shoulders and thighs pressed together on one of the picnic tables.

The final mountain lion was pacing in front of the group, his thin, lanky form all but vibrating with an unknown emotion. Fear? Anger? Nervousness? Other than the tremble in his hands that he tried to hide by wringing his fingers together, there was no way for me to tell.

He jolted to a stop as we opened the French doors and stepped outside. In less than a breath, he positioned himself between his fellow mountain lions and us, taking on the role of leader. He was certainly better-looking than Becker. Young—I'd peg him in his early twenties—and a few inches shorter than Teague, with long, straight auburn hair that flowed over his shoulders to the small of his back. His white skin was pale enough that I couldn't tell if he'd lost some color from whatever emotion he was feeling or the intensity of the frost in the predawn air.

"Are these the people you were waiting for?" he demanded of Teague. "*Now* will you tell me if you'll give us sanctuary or not?"

As always, Teague was stoic. There was no hint that he'd been dealt a critical blow to his emotions a few hours ago. "Not until we're certain this isn't some way to get behind our defenses."

The man swung a hand at his companions behind him. "Do we look like the type that would be involved with Becker's shit?"

"Exactly."

"Fuck."

One of the women clicked her tongue. "Language, Francisco."

Big name for a little guy.

He glanced back at her before rounding on Teague again. "Look, I need to know if we'll be safe here. If not, we're going to have to find somewhere else, quick."

"Tell us why you're here, and we'll let you know," Teague countered.

Before Francisco could swear again, the gray-haired man said, "Tell them. If we want them to trust us, we have to trust them."

Francisco's head drooped between his stiff shoulders, his hands braced on his hips. When he looked up again, some of the fire had fled his gaze. "We're the lowest of the low in the pride."

Logan growled. "Don't tell me this Becker follows the alpha-omega doctrine bullshit."

"Oh, he follows it, all right." He laughed, but there was no humor in the sound. "He's the alpha, his bikers are 'betas,' and then there's us. We're not bikers. We're not important except for, you know, keeping the entire pride running." He pointed to the older man. "Henry's their mechanic—or was, I guess. Chase was their runner. Nikki and Sarah took care of the house—cleaning, cooking."

"And you?" Teague asked.

"I took care of other things." Francisco's look was defiant, daring Teague to push. Teague didn't, which made me wonder what he was feeling from the younger man. "Back before Becker took over the pride, things were good. Then he won the challenge, took leadership—I use that term loosely—and brought in his biker buddies. Suddenly, all the good folks were gone, chased off, and those of us who had nowhere to go and no means to get there were left behind." For a second, his tough mask slipped, and I saw the worry he tried to hide. "When I overheard one of Becker's men talking with some others about the deal Becker had made with the...what was the term? Fomori?" He continued at Teague's nod. "I knew we had to get out of there. If he's willing to sacrifice the pride members he considers more important than us..." He trailed off, but he didn't have to finish the sentence.

"I don't think he's lying," Logan said with a grunt. "His heart rate's steady, if a bit elevated—from nerves, I imagine—and he's not sweating excessively. Again, considering where he is and what he's doing."

"I swear I'm not lying," Francisco said. "I've never wanted anything to do with Becker's plan for Arrington. None of us have. All we want is somewhere we can live peacefully and be treated right. It's not like we're asking you to take us in forever. All we need is a safe place to stay until this whole situation gets resolved."

"Give us a few minutes." Teague gestured at us to head inside, which we did. He led us to the office we rarely used, the easiest-to-access room farthest from the back patio— presumably to prevent the mountain lion shifters from hearing us.

None of us took advantage of the seating. Drew had his arms crossed, and Josh leaned against him. Teague stood at parade rest, a position I wasn't sure he'd consciously adopted. Logan was a pillar I happily rested my weight against—and I was even more content when he lifted his arm and I could wedge myself more firmly against his side.

"I don't know," Teague said finally. "I also don't think he's lying, but I'm not sure I'm willing to take the chance."

I acknowledged his feelings with a somber nod. "You're gun-shy."

He huffed a breath. "Can you blame me? I already trusted the wrong person and look what that led to."

"Allies." Logan's voice rumbled through my body. I

fought an entirely inappropriate shiver. "Despite the circumstances, I honestly believe Christian Holt is still your ally. He did shitty things, and I'm not saying he should be forgiven for them, but you don't have to be friends to work together."

Teague grunted but didn't otherwise react to Logan's words. I understood—Christian and his family was a sore topic. One to be discussed in more detail at a later time. Right now, we had five mountain lions to deal with.

"I say we help them," Josh said. "You and Logan believe them, which is good enough for me. They've got nowhere else to go, nowhere else to find refuge. I wouldn't feel right sending them away."

"You're too soft-hearted." But the besotted expression on Drew's face said he wouldn't have Josh any other way.

"There's a logical reason to take them in as well," Logan said. "Intel. Make it part of the agreement. You provide shelter. They provide knowledge."

I tilted my head back and forth. "They might not have much, being at the bottom of the food chain."

Logan chuckled. "It's the people at the bottom who always have the most. Francisco already said he got info from eavesdropping. I'm sure he's gleaned other bits and pieces. I'm sure they all have. And he said he 'took care of other things.' The vagueness leads me to believe he might have been more involved in the pride's actions than he wants us to realize, but the protectiveness he's showing of the others tells me if he was, it was under duress."

"So you're voting for them to stay as well?" Teague asked.

"If I have a vote, yes. I think it could be beneficial."

Teague looked to Drew, who, in turn, shifted his gaze to Josh. "I don't want to vote against you, love."

"Then don't."

Drew squeezed Josh, resting his cheek against the top of his partner's head for a moment. "I have to vote no. There's so much unresolved, and I feel adding these folks to the mix would be a mistake. It's already complicated enough as it is."

Teague nodded. "Rian?"

Blowing out a breath, I considered the options. Drew and Josh were making decisions based on emotion—which was fair since we all seemed to do that more often than not. Even Teague, because you couldn't tell me his decision to invite what he thought was the MacGrath pack to Arrington wasn't emotional. He'd wanted to give "Christopher" a chance to redeem his family. The help with the pride was secondary since our issues with the cats started well after the deal with the pack had been struck.

Logan's reasoning, though, was based on facts and strategy. Emotion played no part in it. I trusted his thinking more than I did my own in this instance.

"I vote yes," I said.

"Majority rules," Teague said.

I didn't miss how he avoided revealing his vote. My elder brother's confidence had been sorely shaken, and it would take some time to recover.

THE MANSION HAD plenty of bedrooms, but we rarely used more than the ones we occupied. It wasn't like we were teeming with guests. Honestly, we might have been somewhat optimistic when we'd planned and built this house in the late 1800s. We'd recently emigrated to the relatively new country of Canada, and despite the isolation of the

British Columbian wilderness, we had—or at least, I had—felt like it was the new beginning we desperately needed.

The previous time we'd been awake, we'd sailed to the Americas on a doomed ship, which we hadn't known at the time, of course. When it sank, we'd rescued one family: Josh's great-great-great-times-whatever grandparents and their two children. That had earned us caretakers for all eternity, or until we broke the curse. At any rate, by the time we'd made it to New York City, thanks to being rescued by another passing ship, we were less than enthusiastic about our choice to leave Europe.

It wasn't helped by the tensions rising in the British colonies in the lead-up to the American Revolutionary War. Luckily for us, Asger Pallesen was nothing if not a man talented in making money, and he turned those skills toward ensuring his family, and us as statues, were all safe through the Revolutionary War and into the conflicts beyond.

When we awoke next, Asger and his wife, Grete, were gone. The children we'd adored were now grandparents, and there was a new generation dedicated to keeping us safe. It had been the best awakening since the curse began. For once, we were protected, able to ease into the updated world we found ourselves in.

So maybe we'd built this mansion partially for the Pallesens, so they could fill it with children, love, and laughter.

Logan slid into one of the stools beside me at the kitchen island and nudged my shoulder. "Penny for your thoughts?"

I chuckled. "Might need a quarter. I was thinking about this house, and when we started building it."

"It's, what, about a hundred and fifty years old?"

"Good guess. About that, yeah."

"Anything in particular you're thinking about?"

"How big we built it, and why." I shot him a sad smile. "Finnian hadn't met his wife yet, but we'd hoped the Pallesens—Josh's greats—would take advantage of the space. And then, when Finnian broke the curse with Elizabeth, we hoped we'd wake up to great-grandnieces and -nephews."

"I'm assuming that didn't happen."

"Sadly, no. There was a letter waiting for us from Finnian, giving the details of his life and how he and Elizabeth never managed to conceive. Maybe something left over from the curse? I suppose we'll never know since the rest of us will be with men."

"You're pan though. You could—"

I placed a finger over his lips. "I'll be with a man."

He swallowed, his Adam's apple bobbing, and I knew he understood what I was saying. That I wanted to be with him. But I wasn't ready to say that aloud or even do more than hint at it. Because how did I know for sure? I'd never been in love. I knew what brotherly love felt like—trusting that I could depend on my brothers to have my back, no matter what, and to support me when I needed them to. They'd never let me down.

But romantic love? Was it the butterflies in my stomach whenever I caught sight of Logan? The urge I had to constantly touch him? Or was it the need to comfort him and help him solve all his problems, regardless of what they were? Or, possibly, the desire that bubbled up in me whenever I thought of him on his knees in the forest, looking up at me with his mouth full of my stone dick...

Josh and Drew tromped down the stairs from the second level, giving me enough time to withdraw my finger from Logan's lips before they could ask awkward questions.

"The cats are all set," Josh said. "We put them in the rooms at the far end. Francisco—apparently, he prefers 'Frankie'—is in the middle with Chase, Henry's on the one side by himself, and Nikki and Sarah are on the other side. Turns out they're a couple."

"Cool. Finding room was easier than I thought."

"Frankie and Chase could have had their own bedrooms, but someone"—Josh mock-glared at Drew—"didn't want to give them my old room."

"You deserve to have your own space," Drew grumbled.

Josh punched his arm, but there was little power behind it because it barely made Drew move. "I do have my own space. With you. Ninny."

"Where's Teague?"

"Brooding," Drew said.

Of course, he was. My brothers were champion brooders—a fact I wasn't pointing out at the moment since I didn't feel like verbally sparring with Drew. "Holt threw him for a loop."

"Completely." Drew pulled out the stool next to Logan, avoiding the cracked tile. "He tries his best to do right by us, protect us, and he does. Even though it drives me insane."

I raised a stone fist for my brother's human one to bump. "You and me both. But for what it's worth, I think Logan's right. They're still allies."

Drew grunted. "Maybe."

Josh, who stood on the other side of the island after preparing coffee, shot his partner a look. "You've never liked them, even when you thought they were wolves."

"Because they were wolves. Or, more specifically, MacGrath wolves. They are literally the reason Odhrán's dead. I was willing to give them a chance, and I did. And they burned it."

"But it wasn't *them*—"

"Doesn't matter." Drew reached across the granite countertop to run his fingers over Josh's hand. "We can't trust them."

"We don't need to trust them to work with them," Logan pointed out again.

"But how can we have them at our backs if we don't trust them?" Drew shook his head. "I know you think their motivation will keep them in line, but I don't want to stake my family's lives on that."

I understood where both Drew and Logan were coming from, but they were basing their opinions on suppositions—Logan's based on logic and Drew's on emotion, but still, assumptions rather than facts. "I think we need to have a sit-down with Holt and discuss everything. One where we leave our emotions at the door."

"I'm out then." Drew leaned back, slapping his hands on the counter. "I can't do it. I want to tear him a new asshole for hurting Teague. Betraying us. I can't let that go."

It was Josh's turn to reach across the island and Drew met him halfway, twining their fingers together. "I get it."

"I do too," I assured him.

"Maybe it would be best for Rian and me to meet with Holt," Logan suggested. "I'm not sure Teague will be able to leave his emotions at the door either."

"Good point. But cutting him out isn't the best idea. He's the one most personally affected by this whole thing. He should hear the reasoning directly from Holt."

"I don't disagree with you—he should. But is he ready to hear it? Doubtful. And we do need to establish if they'll continue to help us. Uh, you, I mean." He cast a glance upward. "I can't imagine she'll take our new guests' absences well."

My back stiffened. He didn't need to specify what *she* he was talking about. "You think she'll come for them?"

When he looked back at me, his countenance was grim. "I can almost guarantee it."

Chapter 17

Rian

The Arrington Commons was located near Main Street, close enough for shoppers to mosey over after their sprees to rest and relax and maybe snag an ice cream from one of the trucks usually set up next to the river, depending on the season, of course. Seeing as it was December, the truck sold deep-fried pastries covered in cinnamon and sugar, along with hot chocolate and my favorite: mulled apple cider. The air was filled with the delicious scents of apples, cinnamon, and fried dough, underscored by the richness of chocolate, and I inhaled deeply.

The park was busier than I expected. Despite the light snow falling and melting as soon as it came in contact with the ground, about a half-dozen small groups enjoyed the space, particularly the artificial ice rink close to the food trucks. Holiday lights were strewn all around and lit even now in the somewhat gloomy daytime. I imagined at night, it was magical.

As we'd asked, Christian Holt waited for us across the park from the rink, sitting at a wood-and-metal picnic table under a copse of pine trees that protected the table from most of the snow. It was far enough away from the rink to give us privacy for this talk, but not hidden away. I'd chosen the location on purpose—there was no way I wanted him at our house, and I didn't trust him enough to return to the ranch and allow Logan and me to be surrounded by Holt's not-wolves. I also hadn't wanted to meet in the middle of nowhere for the same reason. I wanted Holt to have no opportunity to set up an ambush by hiding his family members around us.

As much as I agreed with Logan that Christian probably wasn't out to hurt us, I wasn't going to take the chance.

Christian stood as we drew closer. He looked much as he always did, wearing jeans and a flannel shirt. His skin looked paler than usual, with dark circles under his eyes lending a bruised appearance, and his lips were rough, with cracked skin and lack of natural color.

He didn't offer his hand when he reached the table—which was good because I couldn't have taken it, and that would have started this meeting off in the entirely wrong tone—but offered a small, closed-mouth smile instead. "Thanks for reaching out."

He sat as we did. We faced each other silently for a second, and it struck me that if we were doing this in a boardroom instead, the scene would feel like any other legal drama. Maybe a divorce proceeding.

"This will be a very quick meeting," I said, my voice low and harsher than I intended, maybe, but this man had hurt my family. "I want to know one thing—will you still stand as our allies against the pride and the Fomori?"

"Yes." He answered without an ounce of hesitation, his voice strong with determination. "On our end, nothing has changed."

The answer I wanted received, I rose, but Logan

grabbed my arm and tugged me back down. "You understand why the brothers have to question your loyalty."

"Yes. *Fuck*, yes." Holt scraped a hand through his hair. "I should have never reached out with the lie. But I didn't know you—your family. All I knew was that at one time, you'd allied with one of the worst packs I'd ever had the dubious pleasure of meeting."

"And they betrayed us," I ground out. "Like you did."

"You're right. We—*I* did." He closed his brown eyes for a moment. I supposed there was no point in him continuing to wear his colored contacts. "I'm sorry for the hurt I caused, and I'm especially sorry I broke your trust. I wish I'd gone about things differently."

I clenched my jaw. "And if the Fomori offers you a cure? What then?"

"Will I take it? Switch to her side?" He met my eyes with his unflinching gaze. "No."

"But your seer said following us will lead you home. What if she's your home?"

He shook his head. "She's no one's home, only their destruction. Look, 'my seer,' as you called them, Keelan, was the person acting as the Moon Speaker. And yes," he added, glancing at Logan, "it was something we made up completely. Keelan is still at the house, and I've been consulting with them constantly. They've warned me more than once that following the Fomori is a path that hastens the fall of my family. So, I will absolutely not listen to any lies she tries to tell me to get me and my family on her side. No."

I wasn't sure how I felt about Holt putting so much faith in his seer, but he did admit he was desperate. Thank the gods Keelan had warned him against the Fomori. I'd take the win.

Holt's gaze ping-ponged between Logan and me. "So, what now?"

"Now, Rian tells you about the guests at the mansion while I go get one of those pastries. The aroma is making me drool. Do you want anything?"

I smiled at Logan as he stood. "I'll have one too. And a cider."

"Got it. Christian?"

"Oh." Holt blinked in surprise. "Uh, no, I can—"

"I'm headed over there anyway, and a pastry isn't going to break the bank. You want a cider too?"

"No, a hot chocolate, please. And the pastry with the chocolate-hazelnut spread."

"See, now I know you're not a wolf." To me, Logan explained, "Chocolate isn't poisonous to us in human form, but I don't know of any wolf who ever developed a taste for it." He bent down and kissed my cheek. "Be back in a few."

We both watched Logan amble toward the food truck for a moment before Christian cleared his throat. "So, you and him..."

"Yeah." My smile fell away. "Problem?"

He was quick to shake his head. "No. Not at all. I'm happy to see you making progress against your own curse. It gives me hope."

"We've been doing a lot of research into it, yeah. Haven't found a solution yet though."

"No, I mean..." Christian's brow twitched. "Granted, my senses aren't what they used to be, but I've got eyes. It's pretty clear you've got feelings for him."

I glared at Christian and wanted to snap back at him— but he wasn't wrong. More observant than I wanted him to be, maybe, but not wrong. "Even if I did, he's not ready. For various reasons I'm not going to get into with you."

"Fair enough. You've got almost two years left. I'm sure you'll figure something out before then."

"Right. Two years." In theory.

In actuality, my gut said it wouldn't be that long before I returned to my statue state. But I had no idea if that meant I had two weeks or twenty months. Regardless, I wouldn't pressure Logan. No matter how I felt—and I had suspicions I didn't want to give voice to yet, even inside my head—I wouldn't make him feel he had to rush into a commitment. No one should be forced into something they weren't ready for, and I knew without a doubt that while Logan's heart was starting to open, it wasn't ready to embrace anyone fully yet. He needed time to heal.

If I didn't have that time, that was on me and the curse. Not him.

I shoved those thoughts away and refocused on the here and now. "We've got some pride members who showed up at the mansion looking for sanctuary."

Christian's brows drew low over his deep-set eyes. "You sent them packing, right?"

"Then they wouldn't be the guests Logan hinted at, would they?"

He sighed. "You know it could be a trap."

"Contrary to the impression we might have given after trusting you, we're not dumb." I rolled my eyes. "Logan didn't sense any lies from them, and neither did Teague. Speaking of, that apology you gave me? You need to give it to Teague. He's the one you hurt the most. And if this soul bonding bullshit you pulled hurts him in any way..."

"It won't. I promise. As soon as we figure out how to save my family, I'll ask Keelan to undo it."

"Why not ask them to undo it now?"

Christian's lips contorted. "It's not an easy spell to

undo. I'd rather be focused on the immediate threat, and I imagine you feel the same."

Again, not wrong. It annoyed me to be at all in sync with Christian's thoughts. "As soon as the Fomori is dealt with then."

"Agreed. You have my word."

"I can't say that's worth much, Chris."

"I know," he said with a grimace. "But I'll earn back your trust and your brothers'. You'll see."

After enjoying the pastries, Logan and I headed back to the mansion. Teague had gone into the station for a shift, but Drew and Josh stuck around the house to keep an eye on our guests. When we entered, it was to find Francisco at the stove, babysitting something in a pan while Drew and Josh sat at the island, the three of them in a conversation about...latkes? The smell of frying potato and onion in the air confirmed it.

"I've never gotten mine to crisp up like that," Josh said wistfully. "They smell so good."

"The trick is squeezing out all the water," Frankie said. "Not some of it, all of it. It feels like it takes forever, so a lot of people skip that step or don't devote enough time to it."

"It's me. I'm a lot of people."

Frankie had tied his hair back—good plan when cooking—and shot Josh a brilliant smile over his shoulder as he jostled the pan. "Well, now you know."

Drew didn't even tense at the expression, so either he'd already established Frankie was no threat or had also fallen under the cat's charm. Maybe both. "So you're going to make these tomorrow too so you can practice, right?" He bumped Josh's shoulder with his own.

Josh laughed, swaying sideways in his chair. "Sure, you carb monster."

"Hey," I called after removing my shoes and leaving them in the foyer. "I hope you're making enough for everyone. They smell awesome."

"Very awesome," Logan confirmed, drawing in a deep breath. "Nothing like fried potatoes."

"Right?" Drew let out a small sigh. "Fried potato *anything*. Give it all to me."

"Glad to know my skills are appreciated." Frankie's happy expression dimmed somewhat, but he forced it back into place. "They'll be ready soon."

"Where are the others?" I asked, settling onto the stool next to Josh. Logan took the last remaining stool on my right.

"Still sleeping. Last night was..." He paused, keeping his eyes on the pan. "It was stressful. I wasn't sure we'd be able to get away from the pride, honestly."

"How did you manage it?"

Frankie's smile returned, but there was a fire in his gaze that reiterated he would do anything he needed to protect those he saw as his. "I drugged everyone, with Nikki's help. I got the Valium and crushed it, and she blended it into the food. See, we prepared a special, more expensive meal for the bikers to recognize their place above us."

Logan let out a low whistle. "You would have had to use a shitload of Valium to knock them out. Unless mountain lion shifters process drugs differently than werewolves?"

"A shitload is an accurate estimation."

"And they didn't scent it in the food?"

"Kind of hard when Nikki added copious amounts of

garlic to the mashed potatoes." He used a spatula to remove the latkes from the pan and pile them on a plate. "Ready for it?"

None of us responded. I couldn't speak to what Drew, Josh, and Logan were thinking, but I was stuck on the idea that Frankie and his friends had drugged people using potatoes.

"Oh my gods, your faces." That brilliant grin was back. "I promise I didn't drug the latkes. Here—what's your name...Logan? You're a wolf, right? Have a smell."

He placed the plate on the counter in front of Logan, who sniffed the food. After a second, he lifted his head and smiled apologetically at Frankie. "They're good. There aren't enough spices in the mix to cover up the scent of anything. It's potatoes, onion, salt, and pepper."

"Sorry."

"It's okay, I get it. But I promise I won't hurt you. None of us will," Frankie said softly. "You're helping us against your better judgment, I'm sure, and we recognize that."

He stood straighter as though a steel rod had replaced his spine. "On that note, like we agreed, I'm willing to tell you whatever you want to know about the pride. Whatever will help."

"Thank you," I said sincerely.

"Why don't we go into the dining room so we can all sit?" Josh suggested.

Josh and Drew sat on one side of our large table with Frankie while Logan and I sat on the other. I hoped it seemed less like an interrogation that way. We were silent for a few moments as everyone topped the latkes as they liked.

Frankie sat back in his chair and looked at his plate. "The pride used to be filled with good people," he said, his tone subdued. "I want you to know that. We're not evil."

"Painting an entire type of shifter with one brush isn't fair, I agree." As Logan spoke, he looked at Drew, who dipped his chin to acknowledge the point.

"Did Becker have the arrangement with the Fomori before he brought the pride to Arrington?" I asked after taking a bite of my latke and trying not to moan from the simple deliciousness.

"The cops ran us out of Prince George, and it was after that when I first saw her. We were holed up in a cabin, and, looking back, it seemed like she was evaluating us, almost. Surveying what she'd purchased. At the time, I wondered how Becker had convinced her to come back to the cabin at all. She's not his type." He nudged his food with his fork but didn't eat. "The next day, he announced we were going to Arrington. There was a place all arranged for us, and we'd have the run of the town."

"How did other people in the pride react when Becker started harassing us?" Drew asked.

"That sort of mischief? They're always down for it. The bikers, anyway."

Josh's turn. "How many are in the pride?"

"When we first came to Arrington, about twenty-seven. After your hacking—which, kudos, that was an awesome move—roughly fifteen, including me, Henry, Chase, Nikki, and Sarah. Now they're down to ten." He grimaced. "She won't be happy about that."

"Speaking of the Fomori." Logan paused for a second, then barrelled ahead. "Does she control your shifts?"

Frankie seemed to wilt. "Yes," he breathed. "Fucking Becker." He put his fork down, giving up entirely on the pretense of eating, and swiped the back of his hand over his eyes. "I haven't shifted in months. I haven't been allowed to. You have no idea what it feels like—not even you, Wolfy. My cat is not a fluffy, patient, pack-oriented canine. He wants *out*, and he claws at me every day." He drew in a shuddering breath. "Normally, we're in sync, you know? He's part of me, my other half. But now I feel he hates me and...gods. You have *no* idea."

"So you've known about her control over the pack for some time," Drew interjected. "You didn't recently overhear it like you said."

"No, you're right. We knew about it. I mean, we couldn't *not* know something was wrong when we suddenly couldn't shift at will. We all thought it was something the Fomori did after the agreement with Becker, without his permission. Knowing he agreed to surrender control of the pride changes everything. He *agreed* to let her torture his people. Who does that?"

The pain in his eyes begged us for answers, but I couldn't give him any. Becker's reasoning escaped me entirely. Even if he didn't care about the people at the bottom of the asinine hierarchy of his pride, surely he had some reservations about sacrificing his fellow bikers?

"Someone who cares more for prestige or money or something else rather than people." Logan's eyes briefly glowed orange. "We need to detach you from the pride."

Frankie nodded. "Yes. Please."

I sensed we were about to head off on a tangent, and I wasn't ready for it. "Sorry—before we go down that route, I've got a few more questions."

Frankie swallowed, then nodded. "Yeah, of course."

"Josh told us he saw a biker riding with half-transformed hands."

"Isaac." The name passed Frankie's lips on a breath.

"I followed him to a fancy mansion on Wilhelm Drive, where I saw him—" Josh paused. "Well, it looked like someone forced his shift on him."

"Yeah. Gods." Frankie grabbed his ponytail and yanked it over his shoulder so he could play with the ends. "That was the Fomori. She was staying at that place because she'd wormed her way into the dude's favor—"

"Martin Garrison," Drew supplied. "The closest thing Arrington has to a drug lord as we can get, according to Teague."

"I knew he wasn't legit," Frankie muttered. "Anyway, she preferred to stay there rather than with us because his place was way nicer. Again, shit that I overheard. Becker never came out and said anything about it."

"So, Isaac?" Josh prompted.

"Every now and again, someone would try to break the hold on their cat. Inevitably, they'd get some part of themselves stuck and need the Fomori's help. Or, well, 'help.'" He made air quotes. "She gave the first few a pass since the restriction was new, but after the third, she warned us there would be consequences."

"What kind of consequences?" Logan rumbled.

"She forced Isaac into his cat and…left him like that."

Logan swore, and I didn't need him to explain why that particular scenario was bad. If he couldn't shift back on his own, Isaac would be stuck as a mountain lion and, I presumed, would eventually forget his human self. I might not be all-knowledgeable about shifters, but I'd been around long enough to hear stories of poor souls who lost themselves in the instincts of their animal form.

Logan pressed his lips into a thin line. "We *definitely* need to get you detached from the pride."

Josh piled his and Drew's empty plates on top of each other. "And how do we do that?"

"It's mostly a 'me' exercise," Frankie said. "I have to renounce the ties to the pride, which will mostly happen in my head."

"But it helps if you have other, non-pride shifters there for support." Logan's gaze turned soft. "My mom told me how she removed herself from her family's pack. It requires willpower, determination, and commitment, and having people there from outside the pride will give you something of an anchor."

"Then let's do it." Josh pushed back from the table and grabbed the plates he'd stacked. "We can wake up the others and—"

His words stopped instantly when Drew's phone rang. My breath froze in my chest. I recognized that ringtone—Drew had set it years ago so he'd know immediately when the police department dispatch was calling him. It was an old police siren, which had been amusing when he set it up. It wasn't so amusing now, knowing that there was only one reason the police would be calling him.

He was Teague's next of kin.

Josh fell back to his seat, his skin washed of color. I grabbed Logan's hand, and he flipped his palm so he could intertwine our fingers. I'd like to say it helped, but I barely noticed, focused solely on Drew as he answered the call.

"Drew O'Reilly." A tiny tremor in his voice gave away the worry cascading through his system. He was quiet as he listened to the voice on the other end of the line. "Thank you. I'll be right there."

"What?" I demanded before he'd even hit the hang-up button.

"Teague's in the hospital. He was stabbed in the arm—"

"*What?*" My hold on my human skin flickered.

"—and lost a lot of blood. I—we need to..." He blinked, looking as overwhelmed as I felt. "We need to get to the hospital."

"I'm driving." Surprisingly, despite his pallor, Josh didn't seem as shaken up as Drew and I, but maybe that was because he was in take-care-of-the-gargoyles mode. Sometimes I forgot he was still our caretaker, even if he'd bonded with Drew. "Frankie, Logan—"

"We've got things covered here," Logan assured him. "Go."

We went.

Chapter 18

Logan

As much as I wanted to be with Rian at the hospital, I told myself it was good I wasn't. Being there, standing by Rian's side with Drew and Josh, would put me in a category I was already too much in danger of slipping into.

Family.

I couldn't be that though. Not when my home was in Victoria, hours of driving and a ferry ride away. Eventually, I'd have to leave here. I needed to put distance between myself and the O'Reillys, and staying at the mansion while the brothers dealt with this new crisis was a good way to start.

I retrieved my laptop and my latest notes and brought them to the mansion so Frankie and his friends weren't entirely alone. The other cats had awoken shortly after Rian, Drew, and Josh left. Chase had discovered a gaming system in the den, and he swore quietly as he played some shooting game. Nikki and Sarah were in the kitchen, poring over a couple of cookbooks and excitedly sharing recipes they found. I wasn't sure where Frankie or Henry was—I couldn't hear them in the house. Maybe they'd gone for a walk. No doubt Henry, as a mechanic, would be interested in the automotive projects Drew had on the go.

It was kind of nice having Chase, Nikki, and Sarah as background noise. Maybe I needed to feel like I wasn't alone either. Despite my worry about Teague, I was able to fall back into research mode, stitching together what we'd gleaned about the pride and the Fomori into a new-ish picture.

I was even more certain now that the Fomori was incapable of taking direct action to kill someone. She had plenty of opportunities to do so—when she'd cornered Josh in the garage, assaulted him, and then set a fire to finish him off. Or when she'd forced Isaac into his mountain lion form, a very dangerous animal who could have turned on her, instead of grabbing a gun and killing him. It completely explained why she'd taken control of the pride—they could act as her weapons, leaving her in the background as they carried out her wishes.

But I still hadn't found a reference to this particular trait in the legends or how to defeat her once and for all. I supposed getting rid of the pride would be a first step, but the brothers had already tried that and been less than successful. Unless they wanted to wage a full-on war in Arrington...but I knew none of them did. I might have been acquainted with them for a short two weeks, but that was clear enough.

So maybe what we needed to do was switch it around. Get rid of the Fomori, and the pride would move on. Fingers crossed. Or...maybe we could get rid of the pride by promising to free them from the Fomori. I didn't think that tactic would work on Becker—he was too invested—but there were nine other pride members we might be able to sway.

If I could confirm a plan of attack on the Fomori.

There was a light tap on the arch between the kitchen and the dining room, and I looked up to see Nikki with a plate of cookies. She held them out. "You look like you could use a break."

I gave her a subdued smile. "Thank you. I didn't realize I'd been so focused..." Momentarily panicked, I grabbed my phone and let out a breath when I saw I hadn't missed any calls or texts. No news was good news. I hoped.

She placed the plate on the table near my elbow. "Can I ask what you're working on?"

"Originally, Rian asked me here to help him find a way to break their curse—you know about the curse, right?" She shook her head, so I waved her to take a seat. I selected a cookie, then held out the plate to her, and she took one with a smile. "Long story short, the same Fomori messing with your pride is the one who cursed the brothers to be gargoyles five hundred years ago. They're awake for twenty-five years, then sleep as statues for a hundred, and the only way they can break the curse is to find their true love."

"The stuff of fairytales," Nikki said.

"Or nightmares," I countered. "They've got two years left of their twenty-five. Drew found his true love with Josh, but Rian and Teague are still cursed. That's how my involvement started. But since I've been here, I've been trying to find out more about the Fomorians, or, more specifically, this one who's causing so much chaos."

"They're from Irish mythology, right?"

I paused as I was about to indulge in a bite of cookie. "Yes. How did you—"

"I took your Introduction to Legends of the North Atlantic course at uVic about five years ago before I had to drop out," Nikki admitted sheepishly. "Don't feel bad about not recognizing me. There were a lot of people in that course."

She wasn't wrong. I rarely got to know my students on a personal level, especially those in the introductory courses. "Of course I'm going to feel bad. I'm sorry, but intro-level courses are—"

"A lot. I know. But I enjoyed it immensely. I always wondered if the Irish legends especially were true legends—they always seemed *real*, you know? Like with the genealogies. How could they do that if the people didn't actually exist?" She took a bite of her cookie and gestured with it. "I mean, werewolves and other shifters are real. Why not the Tuatha Dé and the Fomorians?"

"I'm not sure if knowing that other legends are real is a benefit or not when researching mythology. It certainly makes it harder to take things with a grain of salt."

She hummed in agreement. "So you're looking for details about this Fomori? Can I help?"

Fresh eyes certainly couldn't hurt. Except... "I've only got one computer."

"No problem. I've got a tablet in the kitchen. Let me grab it."

While she did so, I helped myself to another cookie and searched through the reams of loose paper with our notes until I found the one I was looking for.

When Nikki returned, I handed her the paper. "These are legends we found that may be relevant, but either they were vague, or we were tired, or a mix of both, and we couldn't quite determine if they were important."

"You need me to reread them and double-check?"

"Yes, exactly."

"On it. What am I looking for?"

"You might want to write it down." I handed her a pen and a pad of sticky notes. "Mentions of poisonings, particularly by a female Fomori. Stories where a Fomori doesn't take action directly but indirectly, whether through manipulation of people or circumstances. Any references to Fomorians being limited in their actions, specifically being unable to kill their enemies directly."

She jotted down notes efficiently, and I wondered at her story—how had she ended up at the bottom of the social standing in Becker's pride? She was smart and sharp. Maybe that was part of the reason. I gave her the username and password to access the online repository of research volumes I'd been using, and we both dove back in to find what we could.

I lost track of time again until the vibration of the phone in my pocket jolted me out of the zone. The sun had set quite some time ago, by the density of the darkness on the other side of the patio doors. Frankie and Sarah were in the kitchen, their conversation speckled with the sizzling of meat. They were making something with hamburger, garlic, onions, and tomatoes. Hopefully spaghetti sauce? It had been ages since I'd had good homemade spaghetti.

I answered my phone before it could ring again. "Rian?"

"Hey. Sorry I didn't let you know what was going on sooner."

"It's no problem. Your focus had to be on Teague, not me."

He let out a breath. "We're all on our way home."

"He's okay?"

"Yeah. He's okay. They weren't sure if he'd need surgery or not, but they managed to take care of it without it. He's stitched up, wearing a sling, and drugged to the gills. But we managed to convince them to release him. Thank the gods—we were all shitting bricks that they'd find his tail."

"Wait." I blinked. "Teague has a *tail*?"

Nikki glanced at me, her brow furrowing. "What?"

I waved off her question. "Never mind. I'm glad you're heading home. I think Frankie's making spaghetti for dinner."

"Yes!" came Frankie's confirmation from the kitchen. "There will be plenty for everyone."

"Yep, spaghetti," I relayed into the phone.

"Fantastic. Does he need us to pick anything up?"

"Frank—"

Frankie appeared at the archway. "Italian bread would be great. If it's on the way."

"Did you get that?"

"Yeah," Rian confirmed. "Italian bread. There's a grocery store on the way home, so we'll grab some."

"Good. Cool." Hearing Rian's voice opened a longing in my chest, which was so absurd. I mean, it'd been a short time since I'd seen him. There was this weird blend of need and excitement churning inside me, and what I suddenly wanted more than anything else was to hold him in my arms and inhale his stone-and-magic scent deep into my lungs. "Uh. So. I guess I'll see you soon."

"Half an hour at most."

"Good. Great. Drive safe." I clicked off the phone and looked up in time to see Nikki roll her eyes. "What?"

"Thank gods, Sarah and I are way past that ridiculous point in our relationship."

"Which ridiculous point?"

"Where you tiptoe around what you want to say, what you *should* say, because you're scared."

"I'm not—there's nothing—" My cheeks grew warm.

She scoffed but softened it with a follow-up smile. "So, do you want to hear what I found, or what?"

Chapter 19

Rian

"I can scoop up my own damned spaghetti, Rian, Jesus." Teague yanked the thankfully empty fork out of my hand, and I jerked back with my palm facing out.

"Just trying to help." His right arm was in a sling, and seeing as he was right-handed, I'd been attempting to make things easier. Of course, Teague couldn't have *that*. No, no—why would he accept any help after getting stabbed and bleeding out enough that he lost consciousness?

I clenched my teeth and dragged in a breath through my nostrils.

A hand reached around my shoulders from my other side. Logan. He'd practically lit up when I'd walked in the door with my brothers. His eyes had been tender, welcoming, happy. He'd even smiled.

"The spaghetti sauce is fantastic," Logan said, probably in an effort to reduce the tension around the table.

Frankie smiled and swept a stray strand of hair behind his ear. "It's all Sarah and Nikki's recipe. I was her sous-chef since Nikki was helping you."

"I'm glad you like it," Sarah said softly. She barely looked up, but her cheeks were rosy and the curve of her lips illustrated she was pleased by the compliment.

"What were you doing, anyway?" Chase asked after slurping a noodle. "It sounded like you'd beaten the hardest boss in a video game or something, what with all the happy shouting."

Really? I'd been focused on Teague since we'd walked through the front door—maybe too focused—but now, as my gaze roamed past everyone seated at the dining room table, I saw the excitement in Logan's and Nikki's faces. The other cats were content, which told me they'd had a good day. Maybe their first relaxed day in ages. In contrast, Drew and Josh carried tension in their shoulders, the same riding mine. I wouldn't soon forget the sight of my oldest brother lying in a hospital bed, nearly as pale as the ivory sheets. Teague wasn't supposed to get hurt.

It was the first time the nature of his job had jumped up and shouted in my face. Teague wasn't *supposed* to get hurt, but he could. Easily.

"Nikki was helping me go through some of the legends Rian and I had marked to re-examine." Logan was almost bubbly, which was odd and amazing to hear. "I think we found our Fomori."

"Go on," Teague grumbled. Despite insisting he could handle his utensil in his nondominant hand, he hadn't eaten anything. *Stubborn bastard.*

"It's a tale about a battle the Fomorians had with the Tuatha Dé. The night before the battle, the Fomorian king was attacked by one of his people, a Fomori female called Muirloch. There are no details about how she attacked him, or with what, or why, just that she endangered the outcome of the battle. When the Fomorian king returned, victorious despite being greatly weakened, she was sentenced to impotence."

"Impotence? Like, sexual impotence?" I frowned. I didn't even want to contemplate how they'd accomplish that.

"I'm thinking more like ineffectiveness. Such as a certain someone who can't take any definitive action herself."

Teague grunted. "It fits. Though I don't see how it helps us."

"We have her name now—Muirloch. There is power in a name," Logan pointed out. "On top of that, now we know for sure that she has a weakness. We're no longer theorizing she can't take direct action herself—we know."

"*If* this legend is true. *If* she's the Muirloch in the story." Teague let his fork fall to his still-full plate with a clatter. "You don't *know* anything for sure."

Logan's expression dimmed. "Well, no, but—"

"It's more than we had this morning." I glared at my brother. "I know you're in pain and pissed at yourself for getting hurt, but don't shit on this first glimmer of hope, Tadgh."

At the sound of his Irish name, Teague wilted. "You're right. I'm sorry. I'm more tired than I thought." He pushed his chair back, and when Drew and I did so too, he didn't comment.

"I've got him," Drew said. "You can fill them in on what happened."

We hadn't gotten into the details when we'd gotten home, since the spaghetti had been ready and waiting. No one wanted to discuss injuries over dinner.

I settled back into my seat, my eyes following Drew and Teague as they left the dining room. Logan nudged me with his shoulder, taking my attention away from my brothers.

"So?" he asked quietly.

"He was on patrol with another officer when they stopped to investigate a suspicious vehicle on Clarkson Avenue—that's not a great area of town," I explained since he didn't know Arrington.

Frankie winced. "It's really not. Our first clubhouse in Arrington was a few streets over."

"Teague and his partner went to check out the pickup, and as soon as they did, someone popped out of the truck bed and attacked Teague."

"With a knife," Logan supplied.

"No. With claws."

Sarah sucked in an audible breath. "It was someone from the pride?"

"Yeah. Teague said it wasn't Becker or any of the other cats we've seen, and he has no idea if it was an ambush set up specifically for him or for any cop who came that way." I let out a shaky breath. "If he'd been alone, he would've taken on his living stone form, but he couldn't with his partner there. So...he got stabbed."

I didn't resist as Logan pulled me flush against his side. I needed physical support, and I loved that he knew it.

My breath hitched. Logan squeezed my shoulder, probably thinking I was getting choked up over Teague's circumstances. He couldn't know where my mind had gone—what I'd thought to myself.

That I loved *him*.

"If they targeted Teague specifically, that's worrisome," Logan said, oblivious to my internal revelation. "But if they're going after Arrington cops in general...I think that's even more concerning."

"Because it shows the Fomori's focus has expanded beyond the brothers," Josh said.

Logan nodded. "And she's willing to entangle normal humans in her plot."

Frankie's eyes flashed orange. "Well, that's not going to happen. We're not going to let it. Right?"

One by one, his fellow mountain lions nodded, each bearing expressions as determined as Frankie's.

"Right." Logan gave me a final squeeze before pushing to his feet. "Let's get you all detached from the pride and out from under her control. If we've got a war to wage, we need you to be in sync with your cats again."

IN THE END, the ritual to remove Frankie and the others from Becker's pride wasn't much of a ritual. After cleaning up in the dining room, we moved to the living room and pushed the furniture out of the way so we could all sit in a circle, holding hands, including Logan, Drew, Josh, and me. One by one, the mountain lions renounced their ties to the pride, and everyone acknowledged and reinforced their intentions with thoughts and words. We went around the circle twice, and though the theory of it sounded easy enough, the effort of cutting the ties was evident on each of the shifters' faces.

It took fifteen minutes, max, and when we were done, Sarah broke down crying on Nikki's shoulder. Henry, Chase, and Frankie shared a look, and before I realized what they were doing, they stripped naked and shifted.

Their mountain lions were not little. Especially not when they were indoors.

A tail caught the lamp on the table beside one of the

chairs, sending it crashing to the floor. Josh jumped to his feet and started waving the cats toward the patio door. "Okay. All kitties out. Go play."

The cats happily headed in that direction, including Nikki and Sarah, who were shedding clothes on the way. As soon as they felt the cold ground under their feet, they were off, the female mountain lions shifting and chasing them. They disappeared into the forest, barely making a sound, and a weight lifted off my shoulders.

This had been a shitty day, with Teague getting hurt, but this moment? This moment was *wonderful*. We'd done something right. We'd had success. It didn't quite balance out the worry I'd felt for my brother—still felt, if I were being honest—but it went a long way toward making me feel like we could come out of this situation with a win.

I leaned my head against Logan's shoulder, still looking out at the forest though the mountain lions were well out of view. "I think I'm ready for bed."

Logan's chuckle vibrated through me. "It's been a day, hasn't it?"

"Gods, you're not kidding." It wasn't even so much about sleeping but about having time away from all the tumult. I wanted to be alone with him. If he was up for sex, that would be awesome, but I wasn't going to complain if he wasn't. Being close to him would be enough to recharge my well.

We bid goodnight to Josh and Drew and headed for the guesthouse. I wasn't sure when I'd started to think of it as home more than the main house, but I had. The small house was dark except for the lamp we turned on in the foyer, and though I was usually one to chase off the darkness with warm, cozy light, I didn't want that tonight. There was something comforting about the shadows surrounding us.

Maybe because with Logan at my side, I knew I had nothing to fear.

Without a word, I led him upstairs. He also remained silent, content to follow me without question. When we reached his bedroom, I stripped and let go of my human skin with a sigh. As always, the weight of my horns necessitated me rolling my head back and forth to readjust my neck to the burden. After climbing into bed, I turned to see Logan watching me with fiery orange eyes.

Not going to lie. It made me feel amazing to witness his desire for me, despite the horrendous features of my gargoyle form.

"You're beautiful." His voice came out guttural and growly, almost as though it were his wolf speaking.

I blushed and ducked my head. "You don't have to say that."

In an instant, he was naked and sliding into bed beside me. A strong knuckle nudged my grotesque chin upward, so I met his eyes with my red ones. "I don't have to, no. I want to."

"But—"

His strong, huge palm cupped my cheek and jaw. "It doesn't matter what form you're in. I see *you*. The man who's optimistic and hopeful. The man who loves his family without reservation. The man willing to give anyone a second chance. The one who's an incredibly talented artist and who uses magic to make unreal things real."

My eyes dipped to his upper arm, where the tattoo I'd inked into his skin looked like it had been there for months rather than a week. On impulse, I leaned forward and kissed the healed skin. "You can't say stuff like that to me if you're planning on leaving," I whispered, closing my eyes.

"I—I know." Unlike a moment before, Logan now

sounded completely unsure of himself. Caught between his heart and head, no doubt.

I leaned my cheek against his arm. "I love you."

"Ri—"

"Shh. Listen. Seeing Teague get hurt today reminded me that there's a whole world out there that isn't always on our side. I know you're not ready yet, and that's okay. It's fast, but it feels right. At least for me. And if you never get there, that's okay too."

"Really?" Logan's voice was deadpan. "You'd be okay with unrequited love?"

"All right. Maybe not." I lifted my head from the pillow so I could see his face. "But if that's what happens, that's what happens. I don't want to pressure you to say the words back or match your feelings to mine or anything like that. But I wanted you to know. Just—just in case."

In case I fell asleep for good tomorrow. In case the Fomori won.

He leaned in and brushed the tip of his nose against mine before resting our foreheads together. "Thank you. I'm—I'm honored." He sighed, a low, delicate sound. "I'm not sure what the future brings, but I want to see where this goes. Is that...is that okay for now?"

I smiled at him. "That's perfect."

He pulled back, an echoing smile on his face. "Great. Wanna have sex now?"

A bark of laughter burst out of me. "Well, since you're being so romantic about it."

He kissed my nose, a light press of lips, then moved to my cheek. Tilting his head, he slotted his mouth over mine, but the kiss wasn't nearly as good as the ones I'd shared with him in my human form. He quickly moved on, and feeling the softness of his plush lips on my skin, combined with the scrape of his teeth and the bristliness of his beard—it was enough.

More than enough.

I hadn't thought my living stone skin was sensitive enough to feel all the different textures, but Logan ensured I did. He knew to use more pressure than he would on human skin. When he moved to my neck and bit, I arched my head, pressing into the pillow.

By the time he moved down to my hard nipples—beaded like literal stones—I was panting. My cock was harder than it'd ever managed to get since being cursed. Normally it remained perhaps a little harder than half erect, but now...oh gods, now. It was too heavy to stand up, as I remember my human dick doing, so I reached down and helped it lie across my abdomen. I couldn't help but give it a languid stroke as I did so, and my whole body shuddered at the pleasure cascading through me.

"Hey now," Logan rumbled. "No jumping ahead. I'll get there."

"Get there faster."

I rubbed my hand along my length again, but Logan batted it away. "I'm running the show right now." He emphasized his words by nipping at my ribs. His teeth felt sharper than they had a few moments before, and where he held my opposite hip, there were little pinpricks that made me hiss—not in pleasure, but in *feeling*. "You down with that?"

I stretched both arms above my head, surrendering. "So down."

Chuckling, he continued his nipping path, nibbling at the ridges of muscles in my abdomen. His tongue lapped into my belly button, which should have made me squirm, but instead accentuated how close he was to the part of me that wanted his attention so desperately it was doing its best to twitch and move.

When his hot, cushiony mouth fastened over the tip of my cock and sucked, I nearly levitated. His firm grip and the bite of his claws kept me down. Not that I was complaining. Everything he was doing right now was working for me.

Suddenly, he pulled off, panting. A whine escaped me before I could hold it in. "No, why?"

"My teeth..."

"Shit." I tried to sit up, but Logan wouldn't let me. The casual display of his strength and size flared my lust even higher, though it was tempered with concern. "Did you chip a tooth?"

He grunted, an amused sound. "Your skin isn't that hard."

"Then what?"

He lifted his head and bared his teeth. "My fangs are down."

Indeed they were, his canine teeth fully elongated into something resembling his wolf's. A shiver ran through me at the thought of those near my dick.

His expression fell. "I know. I'm sorry. I'm so fucking turned on...it happens."

I shook my head. He'd misinterpreted my shiver for one of fear when it was anything but. "Do it."

"What?"

"Keep going. You're not going to hurt me."

"Are you sure?" He bit his lower lip, which highlighted the presence of those wicked teeth. One pointed end eclipsed his lip, and it was possibly the sexiest thing I'd ever seen.

"Very sure." My hips rolled upward, punctuating my

statement. "I want to feel you…all of you. But I'm probably not going to last." Maybe someday I would, but sex was still too new, too amazing.

"If you do, I'd be disappointed." He licked a stripe up the length of my cock, and I gasped. "Don't hold back. Show me how good it feels."

"Logan." His name left my lips on a broken breath as he licked me again, then lowered his lips over the head of my cock. "Fuck, Logan."

He took me deep, and sure enough, his fangs grazed dangerously against my cock. If I were human, I'd be trembling in fear at the threat to my most precious possession. But the skin covering my dick in this form was the same that covered the rest of me—supple but tougher than it appeared. He wasn't going to hurt me.

He drew back, the suction perfect, then slid down my length…farther this time, until the stone head of my cock bumped into his throat. The pressure of his muscles rippling around me was all it took. I gasped and tried to warn him, but my brain couldn't find the connection to my mouth, probably because all the blood—or whatever it was that ran through my veins in this form—was gathered too far south.

The noise I made must have been warning enough because Logan retreated until his tongue cradled the tip of my cock as the first shot of semen rocketed out of me. He hummed in pleasure as he swallowed again and again, as though I were feeding him the nectar of the gods. The sound and the vibration combined wrung more spasms of bliss from me.

I nearly whimpered as Logan drew back before I was completely ready for him to, but the sight of the last of my spend hitting him in the face more than made up for it. His tongue came out, seeking a taste from the pearly beads in his beard, a sight almost as hot as the fangs revealed by his feral not-quite grin. I couldn't categorize his expression, only that it was possessive, wild, and sexy as fuck. He kneeled, straddling my legs, and my cock gave another valiant but dry spurt at the unbearable provocativeness of the position.

I reached toward the ruddy-headed beast of a dick jutting at me. "Let me—"

"Lie down." Logan's eyes weren't just flaring orange—they were glowing without a hint of his usual human hazel. "I need—"

Suddenly he fell forward, holding himself up with his left hand while the right worked his cock. He stared into my eyes, and I couldn't look away. I felt caged but had no doubt that if I wanted to get up, he'd let me. He might be under the influence of his wolf instincts—whatever they were driving him to do—but those same instincts would never let him hurt me.

I stared at him, reveling in the orange fire dancing around his pupils. If I'd ever doubted I turned him on, his fierce expression assured me he wanted me. Maybe even desperately. Sweat dripped from his brow to my cheek, and I darted out my tongue to capture the drop. His taste exploded across my tastebuds—pine and spice—and I moaned.

Logan bared his teeth in a snarl as he came. His eyes tightened at the corners but didn't close as shot after shot of molten heat covered my belly and chest. For the first time, his eyes strayed from mine to the side, and it took me an instant to realize he was looking at the spot where my neck and shoulder joined.

"You want to bite me?" I asked breathlessly.

"Don't—don't fuckin' tempt me." His voice was barely human. He closed his eyes and grunted as a final rope of come dashed across my skin. Then he looked down and let out a pleased noise at his handiwork.

"You like seeing me covered in your come, huh?" I teased lightly. Figuring my hands no longer needed to be immobile and out of the way, I brought one up to cup his cheek, scratching my talons tenderly through his beard.

"Mine," he growled, his wolf still riding him hard. A moment later, he cleared his throat, and when he spoke again, his voice was closer to his usual human tone and his eyes were no longer orange. "Yes. You have no idea how good you smell right now—our scents intertwined. It's perfect."

"So I shouldn't jump up and go shower?"

That earned me a flare of orange and a growl. "No."

He rubbed the cooling spend into my stone skin. It felt weird, to be perfectly honest, but I wasn't going to interrupt something he obviously wanted and needed. Tomorrow was soon enough to clean up the mess.

I dozed off to the feel of Logan tracing his fingers over my skin, the light touch so good. Soothing. Before I knew it, I'd dropped off into sleep completely.

Until a mountain lion's scream ripped through the darkness.

Chapter 20

Logan

"That's not good."

Understatement. Rian and I moved simultaneously, scrambling out of bed and grabbing the clothes we'd discarded hours ago. Like a werewolf's howl, there was an ethereal quality to a mountain lion shifter's roar that made chills race up your spine. Hearing one mountain lion shifter out there was bad enough, but I was pretty sure there was more than one yowling and screeching. I couldn't imagine Frankie and the others making this sort of noise at four in the morning...

Unless they were warning us.

"Shit, Rian, I think we might be under attack."

"What?" His red, luminous eyes blinked at me. "We're what?"

"That's got to be Frankie and the others making that noise." As far as I knew, they hadn't returned after running into the woods last night—but then, Rian and I had been a little, uh, otherwise engaged. Not to mention we might not have heard them since they would have gone back to the main house. But it made sense. "The pride would be silent until they were on us. The only reason any cat in the vicinity would scream like that—"

"Would be on purpose. Got it."

That determined, I shucked my clothes and shifted. If this was going to be a fight using claws and teeth, I needed to bring my own. We raced down the stairs, burst outside, and headed toward the main house. I let Rian lead since we'd need his fingers to open the door.

I'd made it halfway down the path when something tackled me. The snarl instantly told me what it was, if not who—a mountain lion trying to rake my underbelly with their back claws while their teeth fought to sink through the thick fur around my neck.

They wanted a fight? They'd fucking get a fight.

I flipped upright, my teeth bared, and quickly turned the ambush back on the cat. Like all shifters, they were bigger than their natural counterparts, but then, so was I. True werewolves were larger than the ancient dire wolves, meaning my head nearly reached Rian's shoulder. I was more than a match for a mountain lion shifter. Especially since my wolf and I were completely in sync, unlike these poor bastards who'd been closed off from their other halves for months.

I rushed the lion, feinted to the right, then struck hard at their left flank. My teeth sank through their tawny coat, tearing out a chunk of flesh and leaving a bloody wound in their shoulder. The cat yowled in pain and hissed at me. They tried to swipe at me with their good paw, but their left front leg collapsed under them. I jumped at the opportunity and fastened my jaws on their throat.

"Renounce the pride!" Rian shouted. "You'll be able to shift back to human and escape. Do that, and we won't chase you." He paused and caught my eyes. We couldn't communicate like this, but somehow I knew what he would say next, and I agreed. "If you don't, your life ends here. What'll it be?"

In answer, the cat screamed and brought their back legs up, trying to claw at me.

I bit down and jerked my head away. The cat's throat tore out as easily as any deer's I'd hunted with my mom and brother. I spat the flesh and cartilage to the side and wasted no time looking at my dying prey. They were of no concern now.

"Shit. All right." A shudder raced through Rian, and he released a shaky breath. "Let's get to Drew and Josh."

I followed Rian into the house, reviewing the numbers Frankie had provided the day before. He'd said there were ten members left in the pride. I'd lowered that to nine. I was sure that fact would hit me hard later—I'd killed someone, for fuck's sake—but right now, my wolf's instincts were riding me hard, and I couldn't spare any part of me to care. In a fight for survival, I would always win. There was no other choice.

We found Drew, Josh, and Teague arguing outside a nondescript door halfway down the hallway that led to the brothers' study. Teague was in his living stone form, his eyes blazing purple, and...yep, that was a spade-tipped tail flicking behind him. Wow. He'd abandoned the sling, and there was a dark, angry-looking stitched-up gash stretching from close to his shoulder, down the side of his arm, and ending right below his elbow. It looked like someone had tried to filet his flesh from his arm. He held a pistol in his left hand, making me wonder if he was as inept with his nondominant hand as he seemed at dinner.

Drew held a hunting rifle, his knuckles white as he clutched it hard. He'd thrown on oil-stained jeans and a threadbare black sweatshirt. His blue eyes didn't glow, but if he'd still been a gargoyle, I imagined they would be. Beside him, Josh was glaring at both brothers, looking a little ridiculous in green-and-yellow flannel pajama pants and a matching lime-green T-shirt that read: *Coffee first. Then I'll shine.*

"I'm not going into the safe room," Josh insisted.

"You *both* need to get in there," Teague growled, his eyes flaring.

Drew shook his head. "Fuck that. Josh will, but I—"

"You expect me to sit in there and wait while my family fights?" Josh's glare deepened. "Fuck *that*. Give me the gun, Drew. *Drew*." He clenched his jaw. "You do your metal thing, and I'll cover you. You know I've been practicing."

It took a couple of seconds, but Drew gave in. "I'm trusting you not to get hurt. I don't want to sit beside a hospital bed again, okay?"

Josh grabbed a handful of his partner's shirt and dragged him forward to plant a hard kiss on his lips. "Same goes."

Rian interrupted without apology. "Logan was attacked by a lion on our way from the guesthouse. We offered him a chance to renounce the pack, but he didn't, so...he's dead."

"Good," Teague said coldly. "They think we'll be easy targets, but they're wrong. I called Chris. Backup is on its way."

Glass shattered, the sound sudden and unexpected. I jerked my head in the direction of the sound—the patio door—and bolted, my claws scraping against the floorboards. As I rounded the corner into the kitchen, I saw a mountain lion half in and half out of the patio door, surrounded by shards of glass. More than a few of the glittering pieces had blood on them. Had the cat been that desperate to get at us? Or had the Fomori—Muirloch— forced them to break through the glass?

The lion stalked forward. Their mouth opened wide to screech at me as I put myself between them and my almost-pack. I bared my teeth in response. Crouching, I readied my muscles to leap to meet the cat's attack.

That's when another two crowded in through the broken patio door.

"We'll give you the same chance we gave the mountain lion who fought Logan outside," Rian yelled. "Renounce the pride. You can detach yourself, and it'll allow you to shift back to human. Do that, and we'll let you go. We won't chase you. If you don't, we'll show no mercy."

Two of the cats yowled in defiance. The third, though... backed out onto the patio. I kept an eye on them—until Teague fired his pistol.

Christ, guns were loud, especially to my canine eardrums. My head rang with it, but I shook it off as the already bloody lead cat attacked. I met their leap with one of my own, and we tangled together, sliding across the smooth floor until we hit something hard. The rattle of wood against wood told me it was the dining room table. I snapped at their face while their back claws attempted to disembowel me—but I had back feet of my own and knew how to use them. I kicked at their stomach, digging in hard, but I didn't manage to gouge the skin. Though I did success-fully put space between us, which I took advantage of. Scrambling to my feet a second or two faster than they could, I jumped forward, aiming for their throat. I latched on, and this time, I didn't pause before I ripped chunks of flesh away.

I turned back to the remaining mountain lion, discov-ering they were down as well, blood pooling beneath their still body. A naked human male I didn't recognize stood on the other side of the shattered door, shivering in the cold with his hands in the air.

"C'mere," Drew said, gesturing to the man with a handful of forks.

"You said I could go if I renounced the pride."

"Sure. After we kick the pride's ass. I don't want you out there helping them."

"Fuck. Fine." He gingerly stepped over the glass toward Drew. "Now what?"

"Turn around."

The shifter did so, and I watched, amazed, as Drew pulled the man's hands behind his back and used the metal cutlery to form a neat pair of handcuffs. He grabbed the man by the cuffs and turned to Teague. "I think I know who can go into the safe room, dearthair."

Teague gave a single nod. "Do it."

"Four down," Rian said, looking to his eldest brother. "Six to go."

A tremor in his voice made me look up at him in worry, but I didn't see or smell any injuries. I nudged his hand.

He lifted it to stroke the fur between my ears. "I'm okay. Adrenaline."

I pushed my head against his palm, hoping he understood the gesture of acceptance.

"I'm a little worried we haven't seen Frankie or any of the others." Josh's fingers flexed on the rifle.

Now that he mentioned it, I hadn't heard them in some time either.

Teague's expression grew even more darkly determined. "Let's take this fight to the lions."

Drew returned without his prisoner in time to hear his

brother's declaration. "You sure? Right now, they've got only this point of entry. It's—"

Behind us, the front door flew open, the doorjamb splintering into pieces.

"—defensible," Drew finished weakly.

Three lions pushed through the broken front door. A low snarl alerted me to the fact that another three had appeared at the shattered patio door. Flanking us.

Not good. Very not good.

"Aren't you tired of being under the Fomori's control?" Rian shouted. "You can renounce the pride and get back your ability to shift. If you do that and stop attacking us, we'll let you go."

One of the lions screamed, rage evident in his glowing orange eyes. Becker, maybe? Mountain lion alphas didn't have the same amber eyes werewolf alphas did, though I didn't know why. I also didn't care. He was going to go down along with the rest of his cronies.

Suddenly there were more snarls, this time from *behind* the lions we were facing. Ah, the flankers were flanked.

Chase's voice rose above the growling. "It's us! We're here! Frankie and I are in the front. Everyone else is—oh shit." His voice trailed off into a lion's snarl, so I assumed he'd abandoned his human skin to fight.

I couldn't see what was happening outside, but the arrival of the calvary had captured the remainder of the pride's attention. They'd turned and faced their new opponents on both sides of the house, following them into the respective yards. Maybe the urge for revenge against the pride defectors overrode the orders they'd no doubt been given by the Fomori. Maybe she couldn't control their actions. At any rate, it gave us some room to breathe.

"Rian and Logan, backyard. Drew and Josh, with me. Josh, find a position where you're protected and cover us."

Over all the commotion from outside, I caught the sound of tires on the drive leading up to the mansion. Throwing my head back, I let out a loud, long howl I would've used with my mom and brother to let them know where I was and that I needed them. I didn't expect an answering howl, but I got one. Even though the Holt family weren't truly wolves, the sound calmed a part of me.

The cats were outnumbered. We were going to win this.

"I guess that means Holt is here," Drew commented dryly.

Teague's eyes flared. "Good. Let's show these assholes why they messed with the wrong family." He thrust his good arm into the air. "*Ó Raghailligh Abú!*"

"*Ó Raghailligh Abú!*" his brothers shouted back.

Rian and I raced out the back door and found chaos. Cats fought against cats, and a pair of Chris's wolves stood off to the side, unsure of their targets. I couldn't tell who was on our side and who wasn't. Not by sight, anyway, but by scent was another story. It took me moments to identify Henry, Nikki, and Sarah. They all bore bloody wounds, but nothing life-threatening. With a bark to get the other wolves' attention, I darted forward and engaged the enemy cats one after the other to indicate to the wolves who we were fighting.

They clued in quickly, following my lead. Rian fought beside me, his stone talons digging into flesh as easily as my teeth. He swiped over runes etched into his abdomen, chest, and arms—I didn't know what they did, but each glowed briefly at his touch, so they must have bolstered him somehow.

"This is your last chance!" he shouted into the night.

"Renounce the pride and stop attacking, and we'll let you go!"

"Will you now?"

Though I'd never seen her, I instantly recognized Muirloch—the Fomori. The legends were never overly descriptive of her people, but she matched the *darkly beautiful* statement I'd seen in more than one account. Her ebony hair was almost invisible against the backdrop of the night-black forest. She was petite but curvy, her hourglass figure generous through her bust and hips. I didn't know why, but I'd expected her to be wearing some sort of ancient dress. Instead, she wore medium-wash jeans, tan lace-up boots with a heel, a pale-pink sweatshirt, and a puffy rose-patterned vest. If I'd seen her at the mall or anywhere else, I wouldn't have looked twice. Her appearance was *that* normal.

She stepped farther out of the woods and the fighting paused at the new arrival. "My cats are loyal," she said, her voice dancing with a heavy Irish accent. Her gaze was focused on Rian as she spoke, glittering with malice. "Rian Ó Raghailligh."

"Muirloch."

If I hadn't been watching for it, I wouldn't have seen the slightest flinch at her name. She was not happy about this development. "You've done some—what's the modern term? Homework?"

"Knowledge is power."

"Ah, lad, *power* is power. And I have far more than you will ever know."

"Yet you work through tools, like the pride."

One of the enemy cats' ears twitched in Rian's direction while the others remained tuned to Muirloch. Second thoughts there?

"My pride is so much more than a tool, but yes, they're useful."

Was Muirloch so conceited that she didn't notice the cats' reactions to her reference to them being her pride? The one whose ears twitched backward when Rian spoke now had his ears flat against his head. The other two glanced at each other, which made me think they were checking in to see if that term pissed off the other one too.

"Until they're not."

She laughed, the sound like musical chimes in a minor key. It was disconcerting. "You think you're subtle, Rian Ó Raghailligh, but you're not. Not at all. You think to get my mountain lions to abandon me like you convinced the others to. They won't. These ones are loyal to Becker. Loyal to me. Where I go, Becker follows, and so too do they."

"Like pets on a leash."

Though Rian directed the words at Muirloch, I knew who they were really for—the three mountain lions. I wondered if they'd ever truly spent time in her presence. Likely not, considering what Frankie had told us. She wouldn't lower herself to live with the pride before, so why would she do it now? So, possibly, probably, this was the first time they'd heard her speak about the pride. Her condescending words and tone had to rankle.

Was it enough to make them renounce their connection to Becker?

The lion with his ears laid back retreated a step. After a second or two, a man stood in the lion's place, holding his hands up. "I'm out."

The Fomori's expression darkened. "You dare."

"Fuck you, lady," he spat. "I ain't yours."

Rian kept his eyes on Muirloch but nodded toward the house. "Get inside."

The shifter didn't have to be told twice. He booked it for the shattered patio door.

"Chase him down. Rip him to shreds!" Muirloch screamed at the other mountain lions. "This betrayal cannot stand!"

They looked at each other. If I needed further proof she couldn't control their actions, only their shifts, here it was.

"I will leave you in that form," she roared.

It was a threat too far. Both lions shifted back to men. One bore a significant resemblance to the first lion, who'd disappeared deep into the house. A brother?

"I won't turn on my own family," he vowed. "Not for Becker, let alone *you*."

"House," Rian directed them.

They gave him a nod and retreated.

The Fomori shrieked, rage pouring out of her like a tangible thing. With a subtle movement of my head, I directed the wolves and Henry, Nikki and Sarah to spread out around her. We had her now. She could fight, but she couldn't kill us. Not with her own curse of impotence riding her.

Her eyes narrowed. "You think yourselves so clever. Remove my pride, remove my power, yes? But that isn't the sole tool I have at my disposal." She smirked and leveled her gaze on Rian. "My curse runs strongest in you, doesn't it, little Ó Raghailligh. It goes like that sometimes, ebbing and flowing as the years pass. It takes nothing more than a thought to strengthen it further—"

My stomach sank as I realized what she was saying, and my wolf acted before I thought to. I leaped at her even as I heard Rian cry out. She lifted her arms to protect herself, but my teeth ripped into her shoulder. I had a moment to think *victory!*—until she flung me to the ground with incredible force, her strength beyond anything her petite form seemed capable of.

Snarls and growls surrounded me, then the sounds of flesh impacting flesh, followed by whimpers and yelps. I lay on the ground, stunned, my head spinning and my ribs protesting each breath I took.

After a few moments—at least, I didn't think it was longer than that—human hands stroked the fur of my head. For a second, I thought it was Rian, but then I caught Henry's scent.

"She ran into the woods. Nikki and Sarah went after her, but I don't think they'll catch her—she's too fast. You can shift."

Ugh, but could I? My brain still danced like it was in a competition of who could spin fastest.

"Oh no." That was Chase, his familiar voice full of sadness. "Logan, you *need* to get up. It's...Rian."

I pulled the tatters of my will around me and donned my human skin again. My hurts lessened, as I knew they would. My head still rang as I sat up, my eyes instantly searching for Rian.

It took me a moment to realize what I was seeing.

"Rian!"

Chapter 21

Logan

He was a statue.

Not living stone, not this time. I realized now how different his living stone skin had been from true stone. His gargoyle skin had always looked hard, but it had been supple, moving. Alive. This form was anything but.

He was crouched, bent over himself as though his last seconds had been spent in pain. A snarl twisted his grotesque features. He looked as fearsome as any gargoyle carved to protect a building.

I reached out with one shaking hand, looking to reconnect with him. Physically. Magically. But there was nothing but cold, rough stone and a gaping emptiness where there had once been *life*. Even the scent I'd associated with him from the moment I'd met him—warm stone and electricity—had disappeared.

He was gone. Maybe for a hundred years, maybe forever. The outcome was all the same.

I'd lost him.

"No." The choked whisper came from behind me.

Drew. In an instant, he skidded to his knees next to me. "Rian! No, no, no, no. Teague! Josh!"

I staggered to my feet and backed away as Josh and Teague joined Drew at Rian's side. No—the statue's side. The man was gone. I had to get my head around that. It would be better to think of this figure as nothing more than stone because to do otherwise…I think it might drive me to the brink.

All my emotions were muted. My head was fuzzy, which was strange—shifting to human should have healed the damage from Muirloch's hit. Everything around me seemed distant, as though I were watching the scene from outside my body. Drew, Teague, and Josh holding each other, weeping. Frankie surreptitiously wiping away tears. Nikki and Sarah returning from their pursuit and hugging each other when they saw Rian. Chase trying to look cool and collected but leaning into Henry when the older man wrapped his arm around his shoulders. Christian Holt and two of his wolves, still in wolf form, hovering at the edge of the group, awkwardly witnessing the family's tragedy.

And then there was me, standing alone. Always alone.

"Logan? Logan." A hand cupped my cheek, and I blinked down at Josh. When had he moved? "Were you injured?"

I looked at my chest and arms. I had been, hadn't I? "Yeah."

"He took a good hit from the Fomori in wolf form, but shifting should have cleared it up," Henry said.

"He's in shock." Teague stood beside Josh, and I hadn't seen him move either. How strange. "I can feel it."

How could he—oh, that was right. Teague felt everything. That's why he was such a grumpy bastard. My teeth suddenly chattered.

"Definitely shock. Let me get him inside." Josh tugged on my hand. "Come on, big guy. Let's get you warmed up."

That seemed wrong, somehow. "But Rian..."

"Rian, what?" Josh asked, his voice kind.

"He'll be cold out here."

His jaw clenched, and he nodded, tears welling in his eyes. "His brothers will take care of him. They'll get him a blanket."

"Okay. Good."

We walked around to the front of the house, stepping over the ruins of the main door rather than attempting to avoid the shattered glass of the back patio door still scattered all over the kitchen and dining room. Behind us, Teague barked instructions to both the cats and Holt's wolves, but the details drifted above and over my head like a cloud.

Rather than guiding me to the couch in the living room, Josh led me upstairs. Had I ever been up here? I couldn't recall. He stopped in front of a closed door and pushed it open. Rian's scent billowed out, and I found myself sucking a huge breath into my lungs. It was older, a sign he hadn't been in this room for any length of time recently, but this space had been his for so long that it had absorbed his essence.

Someone whimpered.

"I know, big guy. I know."

Oh. That had been me?

The headboard of a king-sized bed was against one wall, and I didn't need more than a nudge from Josh to stumble in that direction. I fell on the bed, facedown, closing my eyes as Rian's scent surrounded me. Warm stone and magic.

His statue hadn't smelled anything like him.

I vaguely noted Josh draping a blanket over me,

covering me from feet to shoulders. He might have said something about getting me water, but I wasn't sure.

Embraced by Rian's scent, I let myself stop thinking to go along with the fact that I'd stopped feeling.

I HELD Rian's hand as we walked through Arrington Commons. Unlike the last time we were here, it was dark, and no one else was around. The artificial ice rink was empty, and there were no lines at the pastry truck, though its lights were on, warm and welcoming, and the aroma of fried dough lingered in the air. Holiday lights sparkled in the trees along our path, mostly white with a few strands of red and green thrown in.

On some level, I knew I was dreaming, but I didn't care. Rian was beside me, alive, and that made me smile so widely that my cheeks ached.

"That's a good look on you," he said.

"What?"

"That smile."

I ducked my head, embarrassed by the praise. In response, Rian lifted my hand and pressed his lips to my knuckles.

When I looked up again, Rian's gaze had turned serious. "Are you okay?"

My brows twitched together in confusion. "Sure. Why wouldn't I be?"

"All you had to do was admit it."

My frown deepened. "Admit what?"

He shook his head sadly. "You could have saved me."

"No." I swallowed hard, my throat clicking with dryness. "No, I—you don't understand."

Slowly, he untangled his fingers from mine and released my hand. I scrambled to reconnect us, but even though he stood right next to me, I couldn't reach him. "I do understand," he said, his voice growing fainter.

"Don't leave me," I pleaded.

"Stop me." It came out as a dare. A challenge.

"I can't!" I yelled, frustration straining my throat, making it ache.

Rian faded from view, and my heart shattered all over again—a feeling I was far too familiar with.

SITTING on the ground wasn't comfortable, particularly not in the middle of December in Canada, but it was dry, if colder than I liked, and the picnic table was halfway across the patio from where Rian's statue stood. I wanted to be closer to him—to it—than that. I'd taken the blanket I'd found draped over his unmoving shoulders and folded it so I could sit on it. I vaguely remembered telling Josh that Rian would need it to keep him warm, but that had been the shock talking.

Rian was beyond feeling anything.

If I'd hoped for some sign of life in the hours I'd been inside, I found none. He was in the same position he'd been in from the moment Muirloch had strengthened the curse. Crouched, snarling, forever in pain. Eventually, there would be snow, and it would pile on top of his head and shoulders, maybe on his jutting chin, and definitely on his horns. I wondered if his brothers would brush the snow off or let it accumulate. Which option would be the least painful?

I wasn't sure why I was sitting here. It wasn't as though

this allowed me to feel closer to him—being in the guest-house accomplished that better. After the night and day I'd spent in the main house, coming back to myself slowly and painfully, I'd retreated to the bedroom I'd shared with Rian, where our combined scents were even more comforting than his alone. As much as I hadn't wanted to leave the bed we'd made love in, I realized wallowing there wouldn't lead to anything good.

I wasn't sure sitting out here would either, but I couldn't bring myself to go inside. Not yet.

At a quiet clearing of a throat, I turned to see Teague standing a few meters away, a couple of folding camp chairs under his good arm. He'd put the sling back on the one that had been sliced, though it seemed to be healing more quickly than a human's injury would. He was in his living stone, but there was no sign of his tail.

"Thought you might want to get off the ground," he said in greeting. "May I join you?"

"Sure."

I pushed to my feet more slowly than I might have a few days ago. My energy was low, and I knew why—I could feel the mental darkness encroaching, much as it had after Lyle's death. I hadn't recognized it then, but I did now after Rian's attention and care helped to drive it away. When I got back to Victoria—

I sucked in a deep breath as the thought of leaving here caused a fresh spike of pain in my chest. But there was no point in debating my options. There were none. *When* I returned to Victoria, I was going to look up therapists specializing in grief and depression.

Plucking the chairs from under Teague's arm, I set them up. They were heavy-duty canvas-and-metal versions, much sturdier than the cheap ones you could find at discount department stores that always made me nervous. That was one thing I adored about being here: all of the brothers' furniture had been chosen to support the significant weight of their gargoyle forms. It meant I didn't have to worry about whether a chair or a stool would break beneath my girth, a luxury I wasn't used to.

Teague settled in the chair beside me with a sigh. Sorrow dimmed his violet eyes as he looked at Rian's statue. "I wish he'd gone more peacefully," he said quietly.

My throat clicked as I swallowed. "Me too."

He was silent for a few moments as the breeze made the needles of the pine trees nearby *shush* together and the bare branches of the few deciduous trees knock and clack. A bird, goddess knew what type, chirped, and its call was answered by another, farther away.

"Usually, it's like going to sleep," he explained. "We get a feeling when it's about to happen, so we go to the place we've selected as our 'perch' and close our eyes. It's like no time at all has passed when we open them again, but we always wake up to a new world. New history to learn, new people to get to know, new technology to acquaint ourselves with."

"It must have been a shock waking up this time around."

A subdued chuckle escaped him. "You've no idea. When we went to sleep, cars had been in their infancy. Then we awaken to discover humankind has mastered flying, gone to space, gone to the *moon*, even, and had created machines with all the information the world has to offer, small enough to fit in one's pocket." He shook his head in wonder. "People are amazing creatures. They truly are."

"Amazing and terrible. There were also how many wars while you slept?"

He tilted his head in acknowledgment. "True, but there's always been war. Perhaps on smaller scales, but war nonetheless. You can't have light without the dark."

"I suppose." Neither my heart nor mind was eager for a philosophical debate, so I let it go and the silence stretched between us again. It wasn't uncomfortable.

"I woke up two years before my brothers."

"Rian told me. The first sign of the magic wavering."

Teague's gaze was on his brother's stone form. "Right. They know that, but they don't know that it meant I was able to see Finnian before he passed." A small, sad smile curved Teague's lips even as his subdued statement dropped like a bomb between us, dragging my attention away from Rian's statue. "Seeing him so old was painful but good. He'd lived a long, happy life and was eager to be reunited with his Elizabeth. She'd died about ten years before."

"Why would you keep that to yourself?"

"I didn't want to hurt them."

"How would it hurt them to know their brother had family with him when he died?"

Teague grunted in surprise. "You're right."

I made a scoffing noise. "I bet that's been weighing on you, hasn't it? Secrets always do, especially secrets that are irrational."

"Irrational?"

"You know, the ones we should share, but we're too chickenshit to do so."

"Ah."

There was something in Teague's voice, some smugness, that clued me in to the fact that I'd been played. "Did you make up that whole story, or is it true?"

"Oh, it's true. And you're right. It's completely irrational." He lifted his good shoulder in a shrug. "Sometimes keeping those sorts of secrets is more a habit than anything."

"Sometimes it's for survival."

"But is it?" He shifted in his chair so he was facing me more than Rian's statue. "Lying to yourself, trying to convince yourself you don't feel what you do, isn't going to make it go away."

I clenched my hands. "I'm not—"

"Love doesn't care if you're ready. Life doesn't. *Death* doesn't." Teague's purple eyes flared. "Sometimes the world takes choices from you. But that doesn't mean you don't get to make other choices."

"What's the point?" I didn't intend for it to come out as a whisper, but suddenly, I couldn't manage anything more. "What's the point of being on this planet if I lose everyone I lo—" I squeezed my eyes shut at the sudden influx of tears.

A heavy hand gripped my shoulder. "Look, I know it's not the same, but you have me. Drew and Josh. Frankie and the others. You called us your almost-pack, and that doesn't end because Rian's not here. We can be your family if you'll let us."

The assurance broke me. The shield I'd fought so hard to keep around my heart, already weakened by Rian's confession of love, by his care and understanding, splintered. I folded in two as a breath-stealing, wrenching sob worked its way out of my throat.

"It's all right," Teague whispered, rubbing my back, reminding me of how Rian had done the same when I'd shared my grief with him. "Let it out."

So I did.

"I love him," I confessed, my voice choked and hardly recognizable. "I love him so much, and it's too fucking late to say it, isn't it? I'm a coward. Such a fucking coward. Why couldn't I have said it earlier, Teague?"

"It's okay."

"How can you say that? It's not! I could have saved him if—"

"Except you wouldn't have," Teague said. "You were almost there, but not quite, and saying those words to him wouldn't have meant they were true. You needed time."

"But it was stolen from me. From us. Goddess, why? Why do I have to go through this *again*?"

I covered my face in my hands and let it all go. All the love, all the regret, I poured it out into the universe so wherever Rian's soul went while he slept, he'd know.

Stone cracked.

My head jerked up. I couldn't have—it had to be my imagination playing tricks. My eyes sought out Teague's. "Did you hear that?"

He shook his head, frowning in confusion until the sound came again. His eyes widened. "I heard *that*."

"What does it mean?" I was afraid to look at Rian's statue, afraid to let my heart have—no, I wouldn't even think the word.

"I don't know. Say it again."

I knew exactly what he meant. "I love him."

"No, say it to him." Teague inched forward in his chair, almost making it tip.

I stood and ruthlessly tamped down on the way my heart kept leaping in my chest. This might be nothing—I couldn't see any visible damage on Rian's statue. Instead of his stone breaking, it could have been a paving stone giving way to the cold...or something in the woods, or...

It happened again as I stepped forward, and there was no mistaking that the sound came from Rian's crouched stone form. "I love you," I whispered to it. To him. "I'm sorry I didn't say it sooner. Please, Rian, come back to me if you can. Let me say it to you properly."

Another crack sounded louder than the rest. Dust and small particles trickled from somewhere near his arm. Under it?

"Rian, I love you. Can you hear me? I do. I promise I do."

Behind me, I was vaguely aware that Teague had risen as well, but he stayed where he was.

"I'm tired of being scared to feel. I'm tired of being scared to love." I cupped the statue's jutting chin. "Please, Rian, come back to me. *I love you.*"

I put everything I had, everything I'd been afraid to feel, into my voice. For a moment, I thought it hadn't been enough—there was no more cracking, no more sounds of particulates falling.

Then...the entire statue crumbled into dust.

I staggered back as Teague let out a strangled cry. Had we...had we been wrong? Was this a side effect of Muirloch triggering the curse? But as the cloud cleared, I saw...

I saw *Rian.*

He'd fallen to his hands and knees from his crouch, and for the briefest second, I thought he was in his living stone skin. But there were no horns weighing down his head, and there was a definite pink tone to his cheeks under the haze of gray.

I sank to my knees and whispered, "Rian?"

When he looked up, his eyes were as bright a blue as the summer sky, with no gargoyle-red tinge to be seen. My breath hitched at the sight, and the hope I'd been suppressing burst through the mental restraints I'd put on it.

A huge smile spread across his lips, and an instant later,

he launched himself at me. I caught him and held him close as his mouth ravaged mine. His subtly changed scent surrounded me. It no longer had any trace of warm stone. Instead, I inhaled the vibrant, *alive* musk of a happy, human male, balanced by the sharp note of magic.

"I love you," I gasped when he broke away for a breath.

"Ditto. Ditto, ditto, ditto. Don't stop kissing me."

I was about to dive in again when a throat cleared, drawing my attention to Teague. He offered a shaky smile. "Sorry to interrupt, but I—"

Rian dropped to his feet and wrapped his arms around his brother, squeezing him tight. "I woke up," he choked out against Teague's shoulder.

"You did. Thank the gods you did." Teague's voice was as strained as his brother's. "I wasn't ready to let you go."

"I love you, deartháir."

"I know, I've always known, mo deartháir beag. I love you too." He kissed Rian's temple before pulling back and quickly wiping his eyes.

Rian wasn't in much better shape, tears-wise. His had left streaks of mud down both cheeks, so he looked as though he wore the war paint his ancestors might have—or, hell, *he* might have, back before he was cursed. My cheeks were wet too, and I wanted nothing more than to envelop Rian in my arms again.

"You two go on." Teague waved at the guesthouse. "I'll share the news with Drew, Josh, and the others."

"No, I can—" Rian broke off, looking at his dust-covered clothes. "I mean, I'll have a shower, and then—"

Teague smiled and, this time, made more of a shooing gesture. "Go. Have your shower, reconnect with Logan. We'll be here when you're ready."

As much as I didn't want Teague to feel like he and

Drew were secondary, dear goddess, I wanted to be alone with Rian. I could have kissed the elder O'Reilly for his insistence. When it looked like Rian was going to protest again, I held out my hand.

"Rian, love?"

I didn't have to say anything more. Nor did Teague.

Rian put his hand in mine, and we headed toward the guesthouse.

Home?

Chapter 22

Rian

I was *alive*.

I thought about pinching myself to ensure I wasn't dreaming, but being able to move was enough of a reality check. I didn't need to do anything else. There was the hot shower water streaming over my skin. The fact I could scrape my hands through my hair to dislodge the minute stone particles my statue form had left behind when it had disintegrated, never to be seen again.

But the best part, the absolute best, was the man standing behind me, kissing my shoulder and running his soapy hands all over my human, very human, skin.

Gods, if I thought too much about what might have been, I would start crying again. I'd almost missed this comfortable-in-his-own-skin Logan. He was more settled than I'd ever known him to be, perhaps because he'd decided not to run anymore. I leaned back against him, reveling in the heat of his skin pressed into mine, his strength and sturdiness...and the hard rod that had slipped between my thighs to bump my sac.

"I'm sorry I didn't say it sooner," he whispered between kisses.

"Shh. No more of that." I tilted my head back farther, and he took the invitation to nuzzle my neck. I remembered how he'd looked at my neck in bed, with raw want, as I'd teased him about biting me. "Do shifters really bite their mates?"

Logan hummed in affirmation. "It's an old practice that's fallen out of favor in modern times. Mom used to tell me her grandpa warned, 'Once yer bit, that's it!'"

"He didn't."

"He did, and in that exact tone too."

I chuckled. "That's terrible, but I guess it did what it was supposed to do."

"Mating—bonding—isn't something you can undo. There's no divorce between mated shifters."

"That's why your mom didn't want to have a true mating with your father."

"Exactly. She didn't want to be tied to him forever."

"What about you and me?"

Logan's throat was next to my ear, so I heard him swallow. "Would you be afraid if I admitted I've already planned out where I would bite you if you wanted?"

From the intensity with which he'd stared at my neck when he'd marked me with his come the last time we'd made love, I'd suspected as much. Desire whipped through me so fast it weakened my knees. "Afraid? No. Fucking turned on is more like."

By the way Logan's cock jerked between my thighs, I guessed he was too. He made quick work of rinsing me off and toweling me dry before herding me into the bedroom.

I couldn't stop smiling. With the midday sun shining through the sheer curtains, the room was illuminated by hazy, magical light. Inviting, comforting, warm. I felt as though I'd been reborn.

I supposed, in a way, I had.

Logan urged me to lie on the bed, his hands tender but insistent. Not that I resisted. I was perfectly content to be directed to the mattress, stretching out on my back as Logan followed me down, covering my body with his larger one and kissing me breathless. He felt so good against me—rounded in all the right places and the weight of him absolutely perfect. If he'd been another sort of man, he could have used his size and heft against me, but this was my gentle giant.

Which he proved in the next instant, breaking our kiss to gasp, "This okay?"

"Mm-hmm." I pulled his lips back to mine, falling back into the simple but unimaginable luxury of kissing him while we were both naked and without the threat of me turning into my gargoyle form unwillingly.

That would never happen again. No more horns, no more inconvenient facial features, no more stone skin. My humanity was once again mine. Fully and completely.

I didn't even know I was crying until my breath hitched. Logan pulled back and examined my expression as I tried to turn my head. Gah, such a stupid reaction. If he decided we needed to talk instead of continuing...

"Hey," he said, tugging my chin so I would look back up at him. "Did I do something wrong, or is it emotions?"

"Emotions," I choked out.

"Want to stop?"

I shook my head vehemently.

"Anytime you do, say so."

"I know."

I cupped his cheeks in my palms and rose to press my

lips hard against his. At the same time, I lifted and rolled my hips to the side, and he got the picture quickly. It was such a turn-on to be with an eminently intelligent man. He flopped onto his back, and I positioned myself so his stiff cock slid up the crevice of my backside. The heat of him scorched my human—human!—skin, and I couldn't stop the moan from rising up my throat.

Logan watched me, his eyes glowing a faint orange. "I love how you move."

"Yeah?" Encouraged by his words, I ran my hands through my hair, my motions smooth and sinuous. "Like this?"

His hands gripped my thighs. The slight prick of his claws told me how much I was turning him on, but he was careful not to break my delicate skin. "Yeah," he rumbled, his eyes flaring brighter.

"Want me to dance for you someday?"

I'd never explored the idea of sexy dancing, even alone, but I found myself eager to do whatever it took to keep Logan looking at me like that. All banked fire and *want*. I gasped as a clear drop of precum emerged from my cock, sliding slowly to Logan's abdomen.

He scooped it up with one large finger and wasted no time bringing it to his lips. His eyes burned as a low growl vibrated out of his chest.

"You can dance for me anytime you want. Or sit and watch TV. Or read. Or draw. Or anything. I'm so damned happy you're *here*."

With those words, I scrambled over to my nightstand. I needed this man inside of me *now*. Opening the drawer, I froze as I realized I didn't have a potentially essential supply. "Do we need condoms?"

"I know you're negative, and I can't pass on or get anything from you. So need? No. But if you want—"

His words dissolved into laughter as I decisively grabbed the lube and rearranged myself on top of him. "Bare is good. Bare is *great*." I squeezed lube onto my fingers, enough that it overflowed and dripped onto Logan's stomach.

A hiss interrupted his laughter. "That's cold!"

"Big baby."

"Give me that." He grabbed for the tube, but I jerked it out of his reach. "Rian."

"I'm using it." I dripped more onto the other side of his abdomen, accidentally on purpose. "Oops."

"Brat. You're going to waste all of it."

My grin was so wide it hurt my cheeks. "So, stop me."

He surged up and flipped me so my head was aimed at the foot of the bed and I was on my stomach. I was shaking with laughter, but it quickly turned to an appreciative moan as one of his huge fingers tapped against my hole, slicking me up before sliding slowly, so slowly, inside.

I wasn't a virgin to ass play—I'd spent some quality alone time with my imagination and a dildo in recent years, thanks to the magic of internet shopping and the invention of unbreakable silicone. But, gods, being open and vulnerable like this to someone, feeling another person's touch in a place I'd never felt it before...it was mundane and normal, but so, so magical at the same time. The fact that I'd found someone to share this with, the fact I was even here, in my human skin, enjoying it...

The tears threatened to come back, but I shoved them aside. Happy tears or not, I didn't need them interfering with the sensations rushing through me. I could break down with joy later.

I widened the placement of my knees and shoved my butt higher as Logan worked another finger inside me. Soon they were pumping in and out, with the help of more lube, and I knew a single stroke on my cock would be all it took for me to shoot. My dick was so hard it hurt as it swung forward and back with each motion of my hips, riding Logan's fingers.

He grabbed the base of my cock hard, suddenly, and held me still. "No coming yet."

The bite of pain pushed the impending orgasm back down, but I knew it wouldn't take long to get back to the edge. "Inside me. Now."

He chuckled as he withdrew his fingers. "Bossy."

There was the squelching of lube, and then the container landed on the bedcovers next to me. A moment later, Logan was lifting my ass higher, and his impressive cock pushed at my entrance and slid home. Slow, steady, perfect. His claws indented the skin of my belly as he kept me from moving without his say-so.

Not that I could. Every nerve ending in my body was on fire. My brain couldn't process everything. I couldn't think. I could hardly breathe—all I could do was *feel* as inch after inch of him entered my welcoming body. Yes, it stung, but that was only one of the messages my body was sending to my overwhelmed brain, and it didn't stand out any differently from the sensation of being filled with a blazing hot dick, of his grip tightening on my hips, on the sound of him panting and growling as he sank deeper, his lips barely brushing my neck.

"Fuck me," I gasped.

I didn't have to say it twice.

Logan angled himself upward, and I instantly missed his warm weight on my back. But one of his thick, heavy hands grabbed the nape of my neck and pressed me down, and honestly, that possessive, controlling grip might have been even better. I couldn't rise up even if I wanted to—all I could do was lie there and take the pounding Logan was giving me.

And, fuck, what a pounding it was.

Every stroke hit my prostate, lighting up my nervous system like a lightning strike overloading a transformer station. The edge I'd backed away from when Logan grabbed the base of my dick rushed back as inevitable as a freight train barrelling down the tracks.

Fuck, I was going to come. I didn't even need a touch on my dick to do it either.

Someone was pleading in a broken, thready voice, and it took me a second to realize I was making those needy sounds. Behind me, Logan's growls had increased in volume with each thrust into my willing flesh. Suddenly, his grip shifted from my neck to snake under my chest and pull me back, sitting up with me in his lap, impaling me farther on his cock. Now he gripped my throat, tight enough that I couldn't ignore the presence of his hand, but not so tight I had even a moment of fear.

"Do it," I begged.

He yanked my head sideways and sank his teeth into my shoulder.

For a second, the pain of the bite pushed my impending climax aside. Then a hand wrapped around my dick in a firm, tight grip, and I screamed as I thrust into it. My orgasm ripped out of me, stealing my voice and breath. Logan grunted in my ear as he jerked upward into me, as deep as he could get, holding me tight as his cock pulsed with his spend. His hips continued casually rocking in time with his softening strokes against my dick. After a few more, my skin proved how sensitive it now was, and those strokes turned uncomfortable.

Sort of.

"What are you doing?" I let my head fall back onto his shoulder and closed my eyes, trying to decide whether I disliked the continued attention on my dick or not. Logan showed no sign of pulling out of me, and that...that I definitely liked. His spend mixed with the lube and made his motions smooth and arousing.

"You didn't think we were going to stop at round one, did you?" he murmured, licking at the new bite on my neck. The connection I'd forged between us days ago hummed, stronger than ever before. I'd claimed him with it, and now, he'd claimed me. I was sure there was more to it, but at the moment, I could barely feel anything beyond the sensation of Logan's teasing touch on my dick and the gentle in-and-out of his cock in my ass.

"You're not getting soft?"

"Something to learn about werewolves, Ri." I could hear the wide grin in Logan's voice, even if I couldn't see it at the moment. "We have little to no refractory period, especially when we're newly mated."

A harder thrust accompanied his words, and I happily gave myself over to my insatiable mate.

When we ventured through the mansion's temporary front door a few hours later, I was greeted with cheers, hugs, and kisses. Funny how Frankie and crew had settled right into our home as though they'd always been there, and they felt like family. Perhaps because the additional people filled the house in a way we'd dreamed of doing when we'd first built the place.

The little detour Logan and I had taken gave Frankie, Nikki, and Sarah time to whip up a celebratory feast. Okay, it was hotdogs, chili, fries, and nachos—all terrible things but oh-so-delicious. I helped myself to a heaping plate of it all, once again amazed that I hadn't lost this.

Thank you, Logan. Thank you for choosing me.

As though he heard my thought—and maybe he had, or at least the sentiment of it, thanks to our strengthened and largely unexplored connection—he nudged my shoulder with his in the middle of loading a tortilla chip with cheese, taco-seasoned beef, and sour cream. We sat in the living room, the least damaged room in the main area on the first floor. The glass in the dining room and kitchen had been cleaned up, but the bloodstains had seeped so deeply into the wood not even refinishing it would help. No one wanted to eat in there with that reminder so...present. We needed to rip up the flooring and lay down something new, but we hadn't discussed what yet. We would over the coming days, I was sure. And I'd cherish every minute. Every inevitable argument since our tastes were so different.

"You should've seen Henry!" Chase wiggled with excitement in his spot on the floor as he shared what he'd witnessed during the fight, nearly tipping his plate. He caught it at the last second. "It was a one-two swipe against that cat. Marcello. I didn't know you could fight like that."

Henry shrugged, but he had a pleased expression. "Nice to know I can still surprise the younger generation."

"It was so fast and vicious and...wow." Chase settled back and chomped on a chip.

"Marcello," Nikki mused. "He was one who ended up renouncing the pride, right?"

"One of four," Frankie confirmed. "Marcello, his brother Elio, Patrick, and Graham." He looked at his hotdog for a moment, not seeing it, before coming back to himself and biting into it with a vengeance. "We gave them all the same choice."

"That we did," Teague confirmed. He sat on the floor as well, having given up his seat for Frankie earlier. "They brought the fight to us, and we gave them all the opportunities in the world to end it peacefully."

"So...Becker?"

"He was in the group in the front," Frankie confirmed, his lips and nose twisting into a feline-like snarl. "I ripped out his throat myself. Fucking bastard."

Not for the first time, I wondered at Frankie's place in the pride and why he hated Becker so much, but I thought those answers were probably pretty dark, and I didn't want to go there.

"The pride is well and truly gone." There was a lot of relief in Josh's tone, and with good reason—he'd been one of Becker's first targets. Knowing the asshole mountain lions were gone and the friendly ones remained was definitely a good feeling.

"The one thing left to deal with is Holt." Drew's words landed like a ten-ton boulder in the middle of the room.

I raised a hand to rub at my horns—rediscovering they were no longer there. Once again, a thrill ran through me. Not only was the pride gone, but my curse was too. After all these years, particularly this last period of awakening, I'd fought hard to find a way to break the curse, and it turned out, love won.

Gods, I hoped love would win for Teague too. That would be the best fuck-you we could give to the Fomori.

Speaking of... "Not just Holt. Muirloch too."

Henry shook his head sadly. "I thought for sure we had her."

"I *know* I got her in the side," Sarah said fiercely. "I smelled the blood."

Logan waved a loaded chip as he swallowed another. "She's unnaturally strong. I'm not sure even the three of you would have been able to hold her down."

"That's not reassuring," Chase muttered. "How are we going to stop her then?"

"There doesn't need to be a 'we,'" Teague pointed out mildly. "The five of you are free. You can go wherever you want. Do whatever you want. You don't need to stay in Arrington, and you especially don't have to take part in this fight."

Frankie steadied his plate on his lap with one hand while the other reached out to smack Teague on the back of the head. Teague scowled, his eyes flaring bright violet, but Frankie didn't notice or didn't care. I was guessing the latter.

"Don't pull that holier-than-thou, self-sacrificing bull-shit. Open your eyes and see what's in front of you, old man. You've accepted us. More than that, you've welcomed us. You think we don't understand how rare a thing that is?" He scoffed. "As if we'd throw that away. Right?" The last was directed at the other mountain lions.

Sarah nodded shyly, and Nikki confirmed, "Right."

I'd grown used to the fact that Nikki usually spoke for both of them. Unless Sarah needed to share a glimpse into her fiery side, as she'd done earlier.

Nikki continued, "We love it here. Unless you truly intended this situation to be temporary, we'd like to stay."

Henry shot us all a smile. "Me too. Not too many places out there for an ex-biker mechanic."

"Oh, I'm totally staying. This house is sick, and you've got a great selection of game systems." Chase's grin was wide and unburdened—something I was glad to see after all the violence he'd witnessed in his short life.

Henry placed his hand against Chase's ear and pushed his head sideways. "You're getting a job. No more gaming all day, every day."

The teenager's expression fell. "Shit."

"You gotta contribute to the household, man."

"They don't *need*—" Chase broke off at Henry's quelling look. "Yeah, okay."

"We'll figure it out. But I'd love—" I glanced at my brothers, looking for their approval, which they gave with smiles and nods. "*We'd* love for you all to stay."

Frankie's gaze settled on the man beside me, who'd been concentrating on cleaning his plate. "What about you, Logan? Are you staying?"

My breath hitched. We'd declared our love, we'd made love, we'd mated...but neither of us had brought up Logan's plans for the future. I wasn't sure about Logan, but I was scared to. Not too long ago, he'd insisted he'd return to Victoria. Was I wrong in assuming all that had happened over the past couple of days had changed his perspective?

Logan leaned forward and placed his empty plate on the coffee table. "If Rian will have me," he said casually.

Before I could even think about it, my plate clattered to the table beside his, and I launched myself at him, cupping his bearded cheeks and landing a vehement kiss on his lips. "*Yes*, I'll have you. Silly wolf."

He grinned, a full-on smile I'd been seeing more and more. "I didn't want to assume."

"Didn't we fully establish you're mine?" I tilted my head to expose his mating bite.

As I'd hoped, his eyes flared orange. I always loved seeing that flash of his wolf. "And I'm yours."

He wrapped his arms around me and pulled me onto his lap—far too easily, seeing as I was a six-foot-tall grown man. But I loved the laid-back, spontaneous display of his strength. It was a turn-on but also comforting. I could depend on this person for the rest of our lives. No question.

"You've already etched yourself into the most important part of me," Logan murmured. "My heart. Forever."

"Get a room!" Chase shouted.

I dissolved into laughter, resting my forehead against his cheek, loving the scratchiness of his beard on my skin.

"We were having a *moment*," Logan mock-growled at the teenager. I could hear the beat of amusement in his tone.

Chase wrinkled his nose. "Do we have to witness said moment? Really?"

"Consider it a preview. Because, someday soon, I'm going to have this man standing with me at an altar, and you'll all be there to witness it. Because—" Logan swallowed hard. "Because you're my family."

I couldn't do anything but kiss him then, despite the soft gagging noises Chase made and Henry's equally soft admonitions. Logan was right—this was family.

And I was so glad he'd chosen to be part of mine.

Chapter 23

Teague

Two weeks later

I pulled my cruiser up to the mansion, glad to see all the lights off and the drive empty, except for Logan's repaired but rarely driven SUV and the compact car Drew and Henry had fixed up for Chase to get to and from his new job as a mailroom clerk at the *Arrington Daily* newspaper. I guessed my brothers' and Josh's vehicles were in the garage as usual, which meant their guests had departed. Letting out a small, relieved breath, I parked where I normally did—beside the garage, where Drew had laid out a gravel parking pad specifically for the times I brought the cruiser home.

Usually, I hated coming home to a dark house, one of the reasons I despised the swing shift. It meant missing dinner with my brothers and our new extended family and returning when everyone was fast asleep. Despite the clamor in my head from everyone's emotions, their absence enhanced the loneliness that dogged me every minute of every day.

Especially lately.

I didn't begrudge my brothers for finding their true loves and breaking the curse, far from it. I was ecstatic for them. Thrilled they would be able to live the lives we'd all fruitlessly dreamed of for far too long. But as I'd learned over the years, where there was one emotion, there was often the opposite one too. Not always—my brothers and their partners loved without a trace of hate in their hearts—but that was more the exception than the rule, unfortunately.

For me, there was happiness and hope and unrelenting joy. But also sadness, despair, and—I was ashamed to admit—resentment. From the moment we'd awoken that first time and discovered how our aunt had modified the curse to give us hope we could break it, there'd always been a chance for them to succeed in doing so.

Not so much for me. Which stung.

It was a long ago wound recently aggravated by my brothers' success. I was trying to ignore that side of myself as best I could. Hence the reason I'd taken this extra shift on New Year's Eve, specifically so I'd have an excuse not to attend the party. Not only to give this stupid emotional wound time to heal, so I could truly enjoy the sight of Drew and Josh, and Rian and Logan, but also so I wouldn't have to see *him*.

Christian Holt.

It had taken some mental practice, but I no longer called him Christopher MacGrath, even in my head. He was Christian Holt—cursed bear shifter, liar, and betrayer. Those descriptors had taken some reprogramming too. Not too long ago, others had come to mind when I'd thought of him.

Handsome. Warmhearted. Kind. Funny.

The sort of man I wanted to spend time with, get to

know, and maybe share some physical closeness with. Possibly someone who'd understand that I truly wanted nothing more than hugs, casual touches, maybe kisses. Intimacy without sex.

Now I understood that the times we'd shared laughter along with coffee or a meal were nothing more than a ruse to keep me from seeing the truth.

I turned off the car and opened the door. As soon as I did, the lights on the back porch flicked on, illuminating partway to the side of the garage. A moment later, a silhouetted figure rounded the corner from the backyard, and I instantly knew it wasn't either of my brothers, Josh, or Logan.

As though my thoughts had summoned him, Christian Holt leaned against the house, waiting for me to fully emerge from my patrol car.

For an asinine second, I thought about closing the door and driving back to the station. But that would reveal far too much, and I prided myself on *not* showing my emotions, even when I could feel everyone's around me.

Right now, Christian brimmed with annoyance. It was an irritating buzz like a thousand bees in the air, hovering but not stinging. I resisted the urge to swipe at my ear. The sound wasn't physical, but it always felt like it was. Instead, I calmly exited the car, automatically adjusting my Kevlar vest so it sat more comfortably after the change in position.

Rather than saying hello like a civilized person, Christian bit out, "I thought you were supposed to be on light duty."

Automatically I flexed the muscles in my right arm. It had healed well and so quickly that it surprised the doctors —of course, they didn't know I wasn't fully human. As a gargoyle, I might not heal as rapidly as a werewolf or other shifter, but it was still faster than normal. "The doctor cleared me to return to full duty, so I took a shift tonight to help a friend. Not that it's any of your business."

Christian straightened, moving away from the wall. "Sorry. You're right."

Regret bled through his annoyance, and I hated that even more. A few weeks ago, I wouldn't have questioned my ability to read this man or any other person. I trusted my senses, always had. Until *he* came along and made me doubt everything. Did he truly feel regret, or was he boosting that particular emotion for my benefit since he knew about my ability?

The worst part was the doubt that made me second-guess myself constantly and wonder if what I was feeling from the people around me was the truth. Drew and Rian—I knew their hearts, so I could trust their emotions. Same with their partners. But the new members of our family? Chase and Henry, Nikki and Sarah?

I especially didn't know if what I felt from Frankie was accurate, and there was no way for me to puzzle it out on my own. *Frustrating* didn't cover it.

"Why are you still here?" I demanded.

Holt ignored my tone, keeping his posture loose and unthreatening. "I hoped we would get a chance to talk. To clear the air, start off the new year fresh."

I was shaking my head before he even stopped talking. "No."

"Fuck, Teague, why are you being so stubborn about this?" He'd stopped wearing his amber-colored contact lenses, and his brown eyes flared a pale orange...or at least, tried to. The curse he bore muted much of his shifter magic. "Your brothers have moved on and are trying—"

Maybe it was the late hour, the exhaustion that came

after working a full and busy shift, the fact I wasn't as fully healed as I wished I was, or even the mention of my brothers and the fact that they were, indeed, trying to move past Christian's betrayal—but something in me snapped. I slammed the car door shut and strode toward Christian. My skin flickered, but my Kevlar was too restrictive to take on my living stone form. Even so, my eyes must have started glowing because Christian stiffened at the evidence I was past my limit of endurance.

"They aren't the ones you bonded your soul to, *Christian*." I spat out his name, emphasizing that it wasn't the one I'd known him by originally. "I am."

"Keelan said they need time to determine how to undo it."

That wasn't news—Drew had shared as much with me a few days after the battle that had nearly stolen Rian from us. I shook my head at Christian, surprised, yet again, that he didn't understand what he and his witch had done. My brothers didn't grasp it, but I could forgive them for it— none of us were truly knowledgeable about magic, and they were preoccupied with their mates, as they should be.

"You truly don't get it."

"Get what?" he growled. "I get that you're angry, but—"

"The one thing that can break my curse is true love. When my soul recognizes another and theirs recognizes mine." I spoke slowly, enunciating each word, then paused, watching his face for any indication that he was cluing into the issue.

His face paled. "No. That's not—"

I spoke over him. "Tell me, Christian, how is my soul supposed to recognize its partner when it's already bonded to yours?"

Thanks for reading *Stone Skin*! Please consider leaving a review on Amazon if you have a minute.
To stay up to date with Jenn's upcoming releases, be sure to join her newsletter at www.jennburke.com/newsletter.

Watch for Teague's book, *Stone Heart*, coming in June 2023!

Acknowledgments

First and foremost, thank you to my readers who took a chance on this series about gargoyle brothers! The response to the first book in the series has been amazing. I hope you enjoyed reading Rian and Logan's story as much as I enjoyed writing it. These two were so wonderfully soft and squishy, and it was really nice to write a pairing that didn't have a lot of angst.

Secondly, a huge thank you to Becky D for letting me pick their brain about tattooing from an artist's perspective. I wanted to make sure I got Rian's thoughts right when he was tattooing Logan, since I've only been on the other side of the needle, obviously. Becky was generous with their time and expertise, and I really appreciate it. (They're also an amazing artist—I have two tattoos from them and I'm eager to visit them for more! Check them out on Instagram: @beckyd_tattoo)

As always, all my love to my very understanding and supportive family. I couldn't do this without you.

Also by Jenn Burke

The Gargoyles of Arrington

Stone Wings

Stone Skin

Stone Heart (June 2023)

Not Dead Yet

Not Dead Yet

Give Up the Ghost

Graveyard Shift

Ashes & Dust

All Fired Up

House on Fire

Out of the Ashes

Golden Kingdom

The Gryphon King's Consort

The Dragon CEO's Assistant

Chaos Station (with Kelly Jensen)

Chaos Station

Lonely Shore

Skip Trace

Inversion Point

Phase Shift

Jumping the Bull

Must Love Dogs...And Magic

The Sheriff of Shard Hills

About the Author

Jenn Burke has loved out-of-this-world romance since she was a preteen reading about heroes and heroines kicking butt and falling in love. Now that she's an author, she couldn't be happier to bring adventure, romance, and sexy times to her readers.

Jenn is the author of a number of paranormal and science fiction romance titles, including the critically acclaimed **Chaos Station** science fiction romance series (authored with Kelly Jensen) and her fan-favorite **Not Dead Yet** series.

She's been called a pocket-sized and puntastic Canadian on social media, and she'll happily own that label. Jenn lives just outside of Ottawa, Ontario, with her husband and two kids, plus two dogs named after video game characters... because her geekiness knows no bounds.